JURASSIC WORLD
CAMP CRETACEOUS

Published by Scholastic Australia in 2021.

Scholastic Australia Pty Limited
PO Box 579 Gosford NSW 2250
ABN 11 000 614 577
www.scholastic.com.au

Part of the Scholastic Group
Sydney • Auckland • New York • Toronto • London • Mexico City
New Delhi • Hong Kong • Buenos Aires • Puerto Rico

ISBN 978-1-76120-090-8

Printed by McPherson's Printing Group, Maryborough, VIC.

Scholastic Australia's policy, in association with McPherson's Printing Group, is to use papers that are renewable and made efficiently with wood from responsibly managed sources, so as to minimise its environmental footprint.

10 9 8 7 6 5 4 3 2 1　　　　21 22 23 24 25 / 2

MIX
Paper from responsible sources
FSC® C001695
FSC www.fsc.org

The paper in this book is FSC® certified. FSC® promotes environmentally responsible, socially beneficial and economically viable management of the world's forests.

JURASSIC WORLD
CAMP CRETACEOUS

VOLUME TWO:
THE DELUXE NOVEL

Adapted by Steve Behling
Cover illustrated by Patrick Spaziante

SCHOLASTIC
SYDNEY AUCKLAND NEW YORK TORONTO LONDON MEXICO CITY
NEW DELHI HONG KONG BUENOS AIRES PUERTO RICO

CHAPTER ONE

"*Run!*"

Darius sprinted through the jungle, not even bothering to push the branches and leaves out of his way. Hot on his heels were Yasmina, Sammy, Brooklynn, and Kenji. They had come to Camp Cretaceous for a once-in-a-lifetime experience, to camp amongst the dinosaurs of Jurassic World.

And they got that.

But they got more.

A *lot* more.

Right now, they were getting chased by an angry Parasaurolophus. The normally peaceful herbivores were not above chasing away creatures they perceived to be threats.

"Is the Parasaurolophus still there?" Brooklynn said, not bothering to look behind her.

Suddenly, a deafening roar filled the kids' ears as a towering T. rex emerged from the trees. In a flash of terrible physical power, it attacked the Parasaurolophus!

"Not anymore!" Kenji screamed, answering Brooklynn's question.

The kids ducked behind a fallen tree. Darius could hear the chomping sounds of the T. rex and slowly peeked over the top of the log. The apex predator dragged the Parasaurolophus back into the trees, eager to dig in.

"Why are there so many dinosaurs around?" Kenji asked, finally catching his breath.

"It's either your boyish charm," Brooklynn replied, still panting, "or the fact that all the fences on the island are down."

"We just need to eat and rest," Sammy said. "I can't keep running like this."

Darius looked at Sammy and the rest of his companions. They had been on the run for days it seemed, or had it been weeks? This trip to Camp Cretaceous had meant the world to Darius—it was a thing he had dreamed of for years, something he had hoped that he could share with his father. But his father had passed away, and the dream trip to Jurassic World had turned into a nightmare.

Looking back to the jungle, Darius saw something poking out from the lush greenery. A smile broke across his face as he pointed at a barely visible sign that said MAIN STREET.

"There's bound to be a way to call for help on Main Street," Darius said. "And food and everything else. Come on!"

"What happened here?" Kenji asked.

"Uh . . . I'm thinking . . . dinosaurs?" Yasmina replied.

The kids were standing in the middle of Main Street, Jurassic World. Before everything had gone haywire and the dinosaurs had broken free, Main Street was the hub of human activity at the Park. Normally packed full of people browsing through gift shops, eating at restaurants, and watching presentations on all the Park's different dinosaurs, Main Street was now a ghost town.

"Okay," Darius said. "Let's start looking for a way to communicate with the mainland. There's gotta be a phone or something here . . . right?"

The group nodded and split up, searching a gift shop. Not only had the downtown area been abandoned when the dinosaurs escaped, but it looked as if the dinosaurs had ravaged Main Street, too. There were claw marks all over the buildings, and many of the storefronts had been smashed in.

Darius's first stop was the lost-and-found bin

at the gift shop. He figured that someone must have lost a cellphone in all the commotion. But digging through, all he found was a pair of sunglasses, a hat, and then more sunglasses.

"Really?" Darius said, incredulous. "No one lost their cellphone?"

Yasmina held up a landline phone, showing it to Darius. "Well, whatever phones *are* here aren't working. The power's out. There's not even walkie-talkies."

Everyone was searching the shop, hoping to find something that might help them communicate with someone, anyone off island who could rescue them. The closest they came was a portable camera that Brooklynn found, which she figured she could use to document their escape for her online followers.

"Oooh!" Sammy shouted, and Darius whipped his head around to see her looking at a copy of *The Insider's Guide to Jurassic World.* "EDB."

"What's an EDB?" Yasmina asked.

"Emergency Distress Beacon!" Sammy said, reading from the book. "After the first park went down, Mr. Masrani installed one on Main Street. It's battery powered and can send an SOS signal one hundred and fifty miles in all directions!"

"Everybody spread out," Darius said excitedly. "We've got a way to communicate with the outside world, and it's located somewhere here on Main Street! We find this thing, and we can go home."

Of course, finding the beacon was easier said than done. Darius had been awake half the night working on the problem, trying to figure out where the beacon could possibly be. All he had to show for it was a horrible nightmare about Ben.

Ben was the sixth camper who had been a part of their Jurassic World experience. But while they were in a monorail en route to the docks, in hopes of catching the last departing ferry, Ben was attacked by Pteranodons and fell into the jungle below.

Darius had no idea if Ben was alive or . . . He didn't even want to think about the alternative. Ben had been a huge germaphobe and scared of pretty much everything. The idea that he might have survived the fall or the jungle was—Darius shook his head to get the thought out. He and his friends had to concentrate on the now and surviving . . . and finding that beacon!

CHAPTER TWO

In the morning, Yasmina suggested that Darius do something fun to take his mind off the beacon search. Maybe that would help him think of a place to look.

Naturally, Darius's idea of fun was to take an educational dinosaur walk, so that's just what he and Yasmina did.

"Learning new dinosaur facts! Woo!" Darius said, pumping a fist in the air. He ran ahead to a plaque on the "Take a Walk with Dinos" tour and started to read. "Check it out! Sauropods can eat up to twelve hundred pounds of food per day! Obviously their necks helped them cover both elevated and lower grazing levels, but still, that's insane!"

Darius raced ahead to the next plaque, which was all about how creatures use camouflage and how some dinosaurs had developed color patterns that allowed them to blend in with their environment.

Suddenly, Darius stopped reading and looked over at Yasmina. "I know where the beacon is!" he shouted.

"Why are we back at the gift shop?" Kenji asked. "We already looked here."

"We looked, but we didn't *look,*" Darius said.

"Well, that clears it up," Brooklynn said sarcastically.

"We never saw the beacon because it's camouflaged!" Darius explained.

Behind the gift shop, there was a grove of palm trees. Darius stopped and stared, then turned his head and locked eyes with Yasmina. She approached one of the trees and knocked on its trunk. A hollow, metallic CLANG sounded.

"Ever hear a tree do that?" Yasmina said, raising an eyebrow.

The kids instantly understood what was going on and ran over to the "trees." They opened them up, and inside one, they found a hidden panel. Sammy popped it open and found a fire hose.

"There's stuff inside!" Sammy said.

They kept opening panels on fake palm trees,

but other than the one with the fire hose, they all seemed to be empty. No emergency beacon.

Darius turned to the spot where the next grove of "palm trees" should be, only to discover that they had been uprooted by something and dragged off.

Then a terrible ROAR echoed down Main Street.

"We have a problem," Darius said.

"A T. rex lair!" Darius said in a hushed whisper.

He and the other kids followed the roar through Main Street. They scrambled atop the roof of a maintenance shed, peering over a jungle wall that overlooked some of the Jurassic World paddocks—specifically, Paddock 9. Darius knew that Paddock 9 had housed the T. rex before everything went totally wrong on the island.

And from the looks of it, the T. rex was making it her home once more. The dinosaur had been dragging the fake palm trees into the lair, along with real trees, rocks, and whatever else she could find, making herself a giant, mound-like nest.

"They found fossilized nests," Darius said excitedly, "but the T. rex never did this when the

Park was open. We're witnessing new behavior! This is great!"

As soon as the words had escaped his lips, Darius could feel all eyes on him.

"This is terrible!" he said, correcting himself. "She's built her lair right on top of Main Street."

"And it's about to get worse," Brooklynn said. She pointed at the pile of fake trees.

Darius squinted and saw a panel open on one of the fake trees. Inside was a blinking red light.

"Well . . . we found the beacon," Yasmina said.

CHAPTER THREE

"How are you supposed to get to the beacon now?" Kenji asked, crouching down behind the wall.

"Don't you mean 'we'?" Darius said.

"No, because I want to live, and living does not involve me walking into a T. rex lair!" Kenji said, then he got quiet. "I just wanted twenty-four hours where we didn't have to think about dinosaurs, or being left behind, or being eaten, or . . . Ben."

Kenji felt the fanny pack around his waist. It was Ben's fanny pack.

"It was nice while it lasted," Sammy said.

"Hey, we can't give up now," Darius said, trying to rally his troops. "I know it seems hopeless, but there's always an answer. We just have to get out of our own heads to see it!"

It wasn't long before the kids headed back into the gift shop on Main Street. They raided the shelves for all the toy walkie-talkies they could find. Sure, the sets weren't as powerful as the real thing. But for the plan Darius had in mind, they would work perfectly.

Yasmina and Brooklynn were posted atop the enclosure, keeping track of the T. rex's movements. As the mighty dinosaur lumbered away from the nest, Yasmina said, "Heading your way, Sammy," into her walkie-talkie.

Sammy crouched in the branches of a nearby tree as she watched the T. rex thunder past. "The coast is clear!" she said over the radio.

That was Darius and Kenji's cue to sneak into Paddock 9. It wasn't easy, and the two had to half climb, half crawl to get where they needed to go.

"I hate this, I hate this," Kenji repeated.

"There!" Darius said, pointing at the flashing emergency distress beacon. Kenji crawled over to the fake palm tree and tried to yank the device free.

But it wouldn't move.

"The T. rex must've damaged the housing,"

Kenji said. "I can't get it out!"

"We don't need to get it out," Darius said quietly. "We just need to activate it."

The plate covering the beacon was smooth, and Darius needed something to pop it open. Looking around, Kenji saw a large dinosaur tooth in the T. rex's nest, grabbed it, and handed it to Darius.

Darius managed to work the tooth into the seam and had nearly pried open the panel. . . .

Sammy was still perched in the tree when she saw the T. rex approach. The dinosaur picked a branch off the tree from just beneath where she was sitting. The branch was positively dwarfed by the massive dinosaur, and the whole tree trembled as the T. rex pulled it free. As Sammy prayed for the massive carnivore not to notice her, she wondered why the dinosaur considered it important for her nest.

Before she could think about it anymore, the T. rex turned and started back toward Paddock 9.

"Rexy's heading back to her lair! Y'all need to get out of there! Darius! Kenji!" Sammy said urgently.

But there was no response.

Yasmina heard the message over her walkie-talkie and sent another message to Darius and

Kenji. "Mayday! Mayday! Guys!"

If the guys weren't answering their walkie-talkie, then Yasmina and Brooklynn were going to have to find a way to stall the T. rex until Darius and Kenji could complete their task. But how were they going to accomplish that, exactly?

Yasmina turned toward Brooklynn, but the other girl was already gone.

Brooklynn ran across Main Street, carrying a video camera in her hands. She stopped right by the Visitors Center, then pressed PLAY.

The T. rex could hear the laughing voice. It was coming from somewhere in the distance, away from its nest. It lumbered away, snarling, in search of the sounds and maybe a fresh meal.

In Paddock 9, Darius had just succeeded in opening the beacon. There was a switch, and Darius flipped it. The light that had been blinking red was now blinking yellow. And a small display on the beacon showed the words SIGNAL SENT.

Darius could hear the roar of the distracted T. rex and smiled.

"Now we just have to find a place to hole up until help arrives."

CHAPTER FOUR

Darius scampered down the tree from his lookout as Sammy smiled hopefully. "Good news?" she said.

Darius shook his head. "The Pteranodons are nesting on the Eastern Mountains. So that's out," he said gravely.

Sammy frowned and pulled out a red crayon and a Jurassic World kids' place mat from the tote bag she had taken from the gift shop. The map was covered in a sea of red X marks. Sammy took the crayon and scrawled another big X on the Eastern Mountains.

"We can't stay on Main Street, because dinosaurs," Brooklynn said. "The mountains, grasslands, and jungle are out, because dinosaurs."

"And Kenji's penthouse is out, because he's bad at math!" Yasmina said with a disbelieving shake of her head.

"Hey, I didn't think my dad was serious about changing the locks if I failed algebra!" Kenji protested. "That is *not* my fault."

"That's actually *completely* your fault," Yasmina shot back.

"We can't give up yet," Sammy said. "We set off the emergency beacon. We just need to find somewhere safe to hole up until rescue arrives."

"Where?" Yasmina wondered. "It's been *days*. We're out of options."

Darius leaned in, staring at the map. "There's *one* place we haven't tried," Darius said slowly. "But I'm not sure you're gonna like it."

"Are you serious?" Kenji said, stunned. "Didn't we specifically run away from here?"

The kids had trekked back through the jungle, all the way to Camp Cretaceous. When they were forced to leave the site before, the place looked like a train—or a herd of dinosaurs—had smashed through it. But on their return, it looked even worse. None of the bunks or common rooms of the tree house were left intact. Everything seemed to have been smashed or fallen out of the trees. Rope ladders were gnawed on, and the ground was covered in dinosaur tracks and broken junk.

"Just hear me out," Darius said. "There's a stream for fresh water, we've got trees and mountains to protect us from the worst of weather and dinosaur attacks . . ."

Brooklynn stared at Darius, clearing her throat loudly.

"Okay, not *all* dinosaur attacks. But if you were coming to rescue a bunch of campers, wouldn't camp be the first place you looked?"

Darius could practically feel all eyes on him, and as he looked around, that was exactly what he saw. The kids were grinning now.

"And we've even got supplies to build a shelter right here! They're, uh, broken supplies, but we could do it!"

Yasmina leaped up and stumbled slightly. She was still favoring the leg she hadn't injured at the Mosasaurus pool when they had raced to catch the last boat off the island. Shaking off the twinge in her leg and the memory, the young athlete clapped her hands. "What are we waiting for? Let's clear that stuff!"

She took a step forward, but her leg gave out, and the young athlete nearly fell. Then another step, and she stumbled, falling to the ground.

"It's nothing," Yasmina said as the other kids

ran to her side. "I wanted to be on the ground now."

"This isn't nothing," Sammy said. "Your ankle is still hurt."

Darius took out the map and looked at it for a moment. "Based on this symbol, there might be some sort of clinic nearby. We'll go see if we can find anything for your ankle. Just rest here."

Yasmina protested, but Sammy made the compelling argument that she was going to need to treat the ankle with some TLC or she wouldn't be winning any gold medals in track meets. Kenji offered to stay behind with Yasmina to make sure that she actually rested.

"Great plan," Darius said, and then he asked Kenji to start sorting through the rubble for stuff they could use to make a new shelter.

Then Darius, Brooklynn, and Sammy left Camp Cretaceous in search of the medical supply station.

CHAPTER FIVE

Brooklynn was walking ahead of Darius and Sammy as fast as she could. Not because she wanted to be the first one to find the medical supply station—but mostly because she didn't want to listen to her two friends talk at length about dinosaur poop.

The conversation had been going like that for a while when Brooklynn heard Sammy call out her name. "Brooklynn! Brooklynn, wait, we're gonna see if there's dung!"

"Just keep walking," Brooklynn muttered. "They can't make you look at dung if you just keep walking."

As she plodded ahead, Brooklynn heard something that wasn't Sammy or Darius talking endlessly about poop—dinosaur and otherwise. It sounded like an electrical hum of some kind. Brooklynn wondered how that could be, considering there was no power on the island.

"Guys, do you hear that?" Brooklynn asked. But no sooner had she said it than the humming stopped.

"You say something?" Sammy asked.

"I thought . . . It's nothing," Brooklynn said, waving it away. "Must have been a weird bird."

Then Brooklynn took another step and saw something through the trees.

It was the medical supply station!

There was a high chain-link fence surrounding the small concrete structure, and some trees as well. Brooklynn couldn't see what was beyond them.

But it hardly mattered right now, because Brooklynn had found what they were looking for.

Inside the medical supply station, they pried open the doors of the supply closet. The first thing they noticed was that the shelves were stocked with canned food! Brooklynn reached out and grabbed a can.

"Never thought I'd be excited to see canned fruit, but check out all this canned fruit!" Sammy said.

Darius poked his head around the closet and found a crate of medical supplies. With help from Sammy and Brooklynn, he pulled the crate out of the closet—luckily, it wasn't too heavy—and opened it.

"A compression bandage!" Sammy said. "This is exactly what Yaz needs!"

She picked up the compression bandage, only to see that the bandage was really, really long.

"All twenty feet of it?" Sammy said.

There were other medical supplies inside the crate, like more bandages, antibiotic ointment, fever reducers, and cold packs. Darius took what he could, stuffing it all inside a Jurassic World tote bag.

When the kids had finished gathering what food and supplies they could, they secured the door and left the medical supply station. On their way out, they looked around the corner of the chain-link fence. The kids were surprised to find rows and rows of large cages. It was kind of a like an outdoor dog kennel, except there were no dogs . . . only hungry dinosaurs!

"What is this place?" Brooklynn asked.

"It must be a veterinary station," Darius said. "These dinos must have been left behind when everyone was evacuated."

"Like us," Sammy offered.

Kneeling down, Sammy reached a hand through the bars. A Sinoceratops nudged her hand, licking it. Looking around, Sammy made eye contact with two sad-eyed Stegosauruses.

"We have to do something!" Sammy said to her friends.

Darius thought for a moment. They had passed a Sinoceratops herd on the way over to the medical supply station. "If we let her out—" he started.

"She could go be with them!" Sammy said, finishing his sentence. "And eat all the grass she'll ever want!"

Brooklynn wasn't sure this was such a great idea, but Sammy was so enthusiastic. She and Darius opened the Sinoceratops crate, and the dinosaur slowly walked out. It made it about a foot from the crate before it started to munch on some grass.

Darius and Sammy high-fived as Brooklynn said, "Totally what we came here to do. Haven't lost track of our goals at all."

Next, Darius and Sammy freed the Stegosauruses.

They also walked out of their crates and started to graze next to the Sinoceratops.

Whatever joy Darius and Sammy were experiencing from setting the dinosaurs free stopped when they heard the low, hungry snarls coming from the end of the row. They looked inside the crates and saw not herbivores, but carnivores: a scarred Ceratosaurus and a green-skinned Baryonyx with deep-red eyes.

"Predators," Darius said.

"Predators," Brooklynn repeated. "What exactly are we planning to do with them?"

"Well, it's kind of a no-brainer," Sammy said.

"Totally," Darius agreed.

The two smiled at each other, and at the same time, they said:

"Obviously we should leave them."

"Obviously we should free them."

"Wait, what?" they both said.

CHAPTER SIX

"Darius said to sort through the debris," Yasmina directed. She was standing on one foot, trying to pull a broken wooden beam out of a pile of junk. But she wasn't having much luck, and she could have used help. "If you don't do it, and I can't do it, who will do it?"

"Everyone else!" Kenji answered as he leaned against a tree. "Yaz, the best things in life are things you make other people do for you."

Yasmina couldn't believe what she was hearing as Kenji smiled and closed his eyes.

Unable to just stand around doing nothing, Yasmina started to limp away.

"All I have to do now is watch over you, which will be totally . . ."

Something told Kenji to open his eyes, and when he did, he saw that Yasmina was nowhere to be found.

"Yaz? Yaz!" he shouted. "Fine, hop away! I'll stay here! Under the tree!"

That lasted for all of a few seconds before Kenji pushed himself away from the tree.

"I can't believe I'm being noble and going after you when no one's around to recognize how boss that is," Kenji said. He sorted through a pile of debris, looking for some kind of weapon that he could use to defend himself. All he could find was a butter knife, but it was better than nothing.

With a deep sigh, Kenji stalked off into the jungle.

"There you are!" Kenji called out.

Ahead of him was Yasmina, hopping through the jungle using a large stick as a crutch. She had gathered a bunch of vines under her other arm.

Kenji dropped the knife as Yasmina pointed with her crutch at a pile of sticks that she'd gathered, as well as some more vines.

"To move the camp debris, we use the sticks as levers, toss the vines over a branch, and use them to haul the rest of the broken planks and stuff away," she said.

"This looks like the exact opposite of what you're supposed to be doing, which is nothing,"

Kenji said, frustrated. "Can you please just give the tough-girl act a rest already?"

Yasmina glared at Kenji. "Three-time state track champ. Four times placing at nationals, twice in the International World Track Competition. I've competed in rain, sleet, and snow, and each time, I've medaled. What does that say to you?"

"That you're crazy, because running is hard, and why would you do that?"

"I don't give up," Yasmina said. "Unlike some people. But hey, I'm glad you're here."

Then she dropped the pile of vines into Kenji's arms. "Because I need you to haul this stuff through the dangerous jungle. Enjoy."

Kenji immediately dropped the vines and grabbed the stick in Yasmina's hand, trying to pull her back toward the camp.

"We're going back and you are resting, whether you like it or not!" he said.

But Yasmina resisted. She growled and let go of the stick. "You are the laziest person . . . I've ever met!"

"And you're insane!" Kenji replied. "Your ankle is getting worse . . . but you refuse . . . to *sit . . . down*!"

Yasmina tried to walk away to prove she was

fine, but the momentum of her first step carried her into a bush.

When Kenji turned to look at Yasmina, he saw that she was holding her ankle.

"I can't stand," Yasmina said, gritting her teeth. "It's worse. I think . . . I hurt it worse. What do we do now?"

CHAPTER SEVEN

"We can't free the predators!" Darius argued.

"I thought you cared about these animals," Sammy said.

"I do!" Darius replied. "But I also care about going home, ya know, *un*eaten!"

Both kids turned to Brooklynn, asking her what she thought. What Brooklynn really thought was *I don't want to be here for this conversation.*

But what came out was "Do you hear that? Over there? I think I should investigate. Over there!"

"If we free the herbivores, we should free the predators," Sammy said. "It's only fair."

While the two kids argued, Brooklynn heard the mysterious humming start up again. Leaving Darius and Sammy locked in heated debate behind her, Brooklynn walked away from the enclosures and around to the back of the

the fence. Soon she disappeared from view.

"If we can't let them go, then we'll have to come back every day to feed them!" Sammy said, then pulled a can of fruit from the tote bag.

"They're carnivores, not omnivores," Darius said.

"Does that mean . . . yes?" Sammy asked.

"No!" Darius shouted. "That means no! We cannot feed them. The Ceratosaurus alone eats two hundred and fifty pounds of meat a day. Where would you even get that much meat?"

Suddenly, it dawned on Sammy exactly what Darius was trying to say. She put herself between him and the Sinoceratops as it happily munched on some grass. "No!"

"Don't look at me like that!" Darius said. "She's what they eat!" Despite the fact that predators eating prey was the way things worked in nature and nothing was going to change that, Sammy wasn't having it. "If I can't feed 'em, then we go back to Plan A: release them into the wild."

"We're not releasing them!" Darius said. "Why do you even want to?"

"Because they should get to go home," Sammy said. "These guys didn't ask to be here. But they are, and now they're trapped, away from their families. And maybe some of them feel bad about how they ran off without telling anyone, and all they want to do now is go home and say I'm sorry."

Darius didn't know what to say. Before he could think of anything, Brooklynn came running from around the corner of the fence, screaming, "Run! Run! Run!"

Brooklynn's screams were drowned out by the sound of a roaring dinosaur.

Kenji was carrying Yasmina on his back through the underbrush. Panting, he came to a full stop.

"Are you kidding?" Yasmina said. "We're nowhere near camp."

"Maybe someone should have thought of that before she hopped off into the jungle!" Kenji said.

"Well, if someone had pulled his weight, she wouldn't have had to!"

"And now I'm pulling your weight! When are you gonna get it? You can't do anything here, Yaz!"

There was silence for a moment, then Kenji asked, "Yaz? What's up?"

"I'm the 'track star,'" she said softly. "The person my coaches, my team, everybody relies on. But now . . . now I'm not. And if I'm not strong anymore . . . what good am I?"

Kenji took a deep breath, adjusted his shoulders, and kept on walking. "What good are any of us on our own? I mean, I don't know one scary dinosaur from the next. But I'm also someone who knows when the best thing to do isn't to push yourself so hard you collapse. Let someone else do the work for a change, Yaz."

CHAPTER EIGHT

Darius's eyes went wide as a red Baryonyx darted out of the jungle, right behind Brooklynn. She sprinted over to Darius and Sammy as they managed to hide behind a tree near the dinosaur crates.

The Baryonyx didn't pursue Brooklynn, however. Instead, it ran over to the crates containing the other Baryonyx and slammed against the locked doors.

The Sinoceratops that had been grazing raised its head, bellowing at the Baryonyx. The predator looked up briefly, but turned its attention back to the cage containing its siblings. The Baryonyx slammed into the crate again, but the lock wouldn't budge.

As the Baryonyx prepared to make another run at the crate, the kids decided to make a break for it themselves. They sprinted toward the

Sinoceratops stall, only to come face to face with another angry Baryonyx!

Now there were two predators on the outside, with one locked in the crate. Sammy dove behind a large log to take cover, while Darius and Brooklynn kept on running.

Brooklynn hopped onto some crates stacked next to the empty stall, and Darius followed. They got on top of the cage and kicked over the crates before the Baryonyx could use them to climb up.

"Now what?" Darius asked.

"That's as far as I thought!" Brooklynn replied.

With her friends trapped atop the cage, Sammy could only watch. Suddenly, the roar of the Ceratosaurus cut through the tension.

"The Ceratosaurus!" Sammy said, looking at Darius. They locked eyes, knowing what needed to happen.

Darius cupped his hands around his mouth and screamed, "Hey! Over here!"

"What are you doing?!" Brooklynn shouted.

"Distracting them so Sammy can do her thing! Hey!"

Brooklynn thought this was a horrible idea but started to wave her hands and scream, too.

The two Baryonyxes were now snarling at Darius and Brooklynn, their attention focused on the kids.

That gave Sammy an opening to run toward the caged Stegosauruses. She lifted the latch, then raced over to the Ceratosaurus cage, raising the bar on that door as well.

The dinosaurs were now free!

The two Baryonyxes turned around as the Stegosauruses and Ceratosaurus approached.

Sammy waved to Darius and Brooklynn as they lowered themselves from the top of the Sinoceratops enclosure and ran toward the front entrance, toward the jungle.

Darius was almost there when he heard a desperate howl coming from a crate.

It was the lone Baryonyx.

"We can't leave her," Darius said. "They're family."

Brooklynn couldn't believe her eyes as Darius turned around and headed back to the crate. He lifted the latch, and the Baryonyx ran out and joined its siblings.

"Aw, that's kinda cute, actually," Sammy started to say as the Ceratosaurus suddenly charged at the Baryonyxes and the herbivores. It was a full-on dinosaur stampede, and it was heading right for the kids!

"Not cute, not cute at all!" Sammy yelled.

The kids turned around and ran into the jungle as fast as they could.

CHAPTER NINE

Yasmina could scarcely believe it. While she rested, Kenji actually—GASP!—did some work! He asked her about her idea of using the sticks as levers and the vines to haul debris away and actually made some progress. He managed to haul a good chunk of debris to the side and make a big firepit. There were even places for each of the kids to sit!

"Welcome to Camp Kenji!"

Yasmina smiled as she watched Kenji proudly admire his work. Then she turned her head. "Wait. Do you hear that?" she said.

Loud footsteps filled the jungle air as Sammy, Brooklynn, and Darius ran into camp, waving their arms wildly.

"The trees—quick!" Brooklynn screamed.

At once, the kids jumped into the branches of a large tree as the stampeding herd of dinosaurs thundered into camp.

They plowed right through Kenji's carefully constructed fire pit and kept on going.

"This is exactly why you should never work on anything ever!" Kenji proclaimed.

"I guess this is why they built the camp up in the trees," Sammy said.

A light bulb went off in Darius's head. "Maybe our new shelter should be a tree house?"

"Maybe something like . . . this?" Yasmina said. She grabbed the map and red crayon from Sammy and flipped the paper over. She sketched away for a few seconds, then held up a hastily drawn picture of a tree house.

"It's great!" Darius said. "Oh, but we definitely need a lookout tower."

"And an awesome girls' bunk," Brooklynn said. "The boys can have whatever."

"A place for storing food so the dinos don't get it!" Sammy added.

"Tire swings!" Kenji shouted. "Maybe a fire pole?"

For the first time in a while, Yasmina smiled.

"I thought you might want this," Sammy said. She walked over to Darius and handed a notebook to him. Darius had seen it at the medical supply shed. "For writing down all the new dinosaur behavior. And I found . . . this."

Sammy held out her hand and opened it, revealing a necklace with a Raptor's tooth hanging from it.

The necklace that Darius's dad had given to him. The one he thought had been lost forever in the carnage of Camp Cretaceous.

Sammy had found it while cleaning up the camp.

Darius's eyes filled with tears as he put the necklace back on, then hugged Sammy.

"Looks like we need some more vines!" Yasmina called out.

"On it!" Brooklynn said, and she hustled out of camp to track some down.

As she wandered into the jungle, she grabbed vines hanging from a tree. After a while, she heard a humming sound—the same humming sound she'd heard before.

"It's back," she said to herself.

She pushed ahead into the jungle, following the humming sound. As she shoved tree branches out of her way, Brooklynn was stunned at the sight she found.

Right in front of her was a small square patch of wildflowers.

Frozen wildflowers.

Astonished, Brooklynn reached down and touched one of the frozen flower petals. It broke off and fell to the ground.

"Ahhh!" Kenji screamed. "Does this water ever get warm?!"

He was standing in the makeshift shower the kids had cobbled together, which was inside the makeshift tree house the kids had also cobbled together. The shower door came from a demolished 6x4, and a water jug was rigged above to dispense water.

Except the water came from the river, which was still cold.

It had been several weeks since Brooklynn had found the frozen flowers, and the group had resurrected Camp Cretaceous. Sort of. The tree house was essentially a big platform sitting in a tree, with a roof over it. There were sheets nailed up to give the campers some privacy while they slept.

Yasmina had just finished her morning exercises when she stepped around a sleepy Brooklynn, who moaned, "Five more minutes." Sliding down a bamboo pole like a firefighter,

Yasmina landed on the ground. The splint she wore on her left ankle was really helping. For the first time in weeks, her ankle didn't hurt!

She approached a tree that had multiple hash marks carved into the bark. Picking up a fossilized Pteranodon claw, Yasmina made another hash mark, keeping track of the days they'd been awaiting rescue.

Darius was sitting with his nose buried in the notebook Sammy had given him, writing away. That's when an empty water jug flew past his face, bouncing along the ground.

"No más agua!" Kenji called out from the shower. "Little help!"

"I got ya, Kenj," Darius said, and picked up the jug, heading to the river.

"If you keep doing that for him, he'll never learn to do it himself," Yasmina half joked.

Darius was about to dip the jug into the river when he noticed a slight problem.

"Uh, guys?" he said as his friends approached the riverbed.

"Where'd all the water go?" Sammy asked.

Sure enough, there was almost no water running in the riverbed. There was only a trickle.

"Shhhh!" Brooklynn said, shushing everyone. "I hear that hum again! The river must have been drowning it out before. If I can follow that sound,

I bet I can find that—"

"'Frozen patch of flowers'!" the other kids said in unison.

"Oh, I've . . . mentioned it, huh?" Brooklynn said sheepishly.

"A few hundred times," Kenji offered.

Brooklynn crossed her arms defensively. "Sorry for wanting to get to the bottom of all the weirdness on this island!" she said.

Sammy raised her hand. "If you're going to look for the noise, I'll come too! It'll be fun to have an adventure for a fun reason—and not a 'fleeing dinosaurs and facing imminent death' reason."

"I'll go if Sammy is!" Yasmina said, her voice full of enthusiasm. "I've been going stir-crazy. Me and my ankle are ready for some adventure."

Clapping her hands, Sammy said, "It's a Camp Cretaceous girl adventure!"

Darius smiled. "And while you do that, Kenji and I will go figure out why the river stopped!"

"Sorry, Kenji do what now?" Kenji asked.

The two groups prepared for their adventures, mostly by picking out their makeshift weapons.

Yasmina called the spear, which was awesome. That left Kenji with the butter knife.

That was less awesome.

CHAPTER TEN

Darius and Kenji had been walking through the jungle for a while, trying to trace the source of the water problem. Something caught Darius's eye, and he ran ahead.

"Dinosaurs sometimes compete over geothermal vents to use as incubation chambers for their eggs!" Darius said excitedly. "See?" he added, pointing at a dirt mound with moist, warm steam rising from it.

"Dirt and steam may be never-ending sources of wonder for you, but my standards are a little higher," Kenji said.

"I feel bad for you," Darius said, shaking his head. "You can't see what makes this place so amazing."

"I *have* seen it all," Kenji said. "All of it. Like a gazillion times. How do you think Jurassic Spa powers its sauna? 'Our geothermal pumps transfer heat from the ground directly to our steam room.' Tour for my eleventh birthday."

Then to show just how well he knew Jurassic World, Kenji pushed a fern that was growing out of a tree side, revealing a hidden speaker.

"Just there to hide speakers," Kenji said. "Sorry bro, but I am *way* over Isla Nublar."

Darius sighed and kept pushing ahead through some plants. The boys soon arrived at a sheer rock wall. Darius noticed a trickle of water cascading down the rocks.

"It's a waterfall," he said. "Or should be. You know what this means—who's up for some rock climbing?"

CHAPTER ELEVEN

"I think this is the place!" Brooklynn said, holding her hand up. The other girls ran ahead to catch up to their friend.

"I don't see any frozen flowers," Yasmina said quietly.

"But there are a bunch of regular flowers," Sammy said, pointing to a small patch colorful wildflowers. "So we're halfway there!"

"I thought for sure—" Brooklynn started, but she was interrupted by a loud WHIRRING sound that came from the flowers! They swayed along with the whirring noise.

"The hum!" Sammy said, surprised.

Brooklynn leaned down, sticking her head above the flowers. "It's . . . super-cold air. And the ground's . . . vibrating!"

As Sammy and Yasmina leaned in, Brooklynn carefully parted the flowers, revealing a metal vent in the jungle floor.

"I told you!" Brooklynn shouted. "It was here the whole time! Who put it here? What's powering it? This place just keeps getting weirder and weirder."

"YazYazYaz!" Sammy interjected. "This is *just* like that episode where Esther follows that graffiti trail." Turning to Brooklynn, she added, "Sorry. Yaz and I were talking before about this show we love called—"

"*Esther Stone: High School PI,* episode 23—when she exposed the cryptocurrency ring," Brooklynn said without missing a beat.

"No. Way!" Sammy said, smiling. "You watch *Esther Stone*?"

"Do I watch *Esther Stone*? I've seen every episode like eighty times!" Brooklynn said.

"Then what are we waiting for?" Sammy said, putting her arms around Yasmina and Brooklynn. "It's time to investigate—"

"A Stone-cold mystery!" Yasmina and Brooklynn shouted together.

"Spread out! See if you can feel any more vibrations," Brooklynn said.

The girls fanned out across the area, then Yasmina suddenly stopped. "I hear something," she said.

Looking off in the distance, the girls could hear a faint hum. They followed the sound.

"That was . . . so great," Darius said, out of breath.

They had just climbed the cliff and collapsed on their backs, exhausted.

"Yeah," Kenji agreed sarcastically, panting. "Who needs . . . actual enjoyment . . . when you have . . . that?"

After a brief rest, the boys resumed their journey, walking along the riverbed. They came to a large tree that was lying across the width of the river, with leaves and rocks packed beneath like a makeshift dam.

"Okay," Darius said. "So all we have to do is move that tree and we should be good to go!"

Kenji gave Darius a look that said "That sounds a lot like work, and Kenji don't do work."

The boys maneuvered around the tree and got a good grip. First they tried to push the tree. Then they pulled it. Lifting was next. But nothing they did moved the tree even an inch.

"Huh. Thought that'd be easier," Darius said.

All at once, the ground began to shake. Darius and Kenji exchanged looks as two Stegosauruses emerged from the jungle! They were fighting, bellowing, and thrashing their tails at one another.

The boys scrambled around the fallen tree as a Stegosaurus tail swung past, smashing into the tree, sending splinters flying everywhere.

Darius saw a small trickle of water spilling around the broken edge of the tree.

"I know how to fix our water problem!" Darius said, smiling.

"What?" Kenji said, terrified. "No, no, Darius, don't—"

But it was too late. Darius was running toward the tree. He stopped right in front of it and flailed his arms. "Hey! Over here!" he called.

Kenji sprinted for Darius as the Stegosauruses continued to fight. They didn't even seem to notice Darius. But they certainly noticed when Kenji whistled. Immediately, the Stegosauruses looked up, braying . . . and charged right at the boys.

Darius and Kenji stood their ground, waiting . . . waiting . . . waiting for just the right moment to run. As soon as they moved, a Stegosaurus followed, its tail smashing through the fallen tree. Water surged through the broken dam.

"We got it!" Darius said proudly.

"Great!" Kenji said, pointing at the still-charging

Stegosaurus. "Now how do we get rid of it?"

The girls had been following the humming sound for a while when they pushed through a stand of trees. The humming grew louder until they traced it to the source—a remote genetics lab.

"Dr. Wu's lab," Sammy said. "Do ya think . . . ?"

"Mantah Corp, Indominus rex, the hum . . . it all connects here," Brooklynn said. "Dr. Wu was up to something big, something secret. And that something must be located right in his private office!"

The trio wasted no time in entering the genetics lab, but when they got inside Dr. Wu's office, they were shocked to find . . . nothing. The room had been completely stripped. There were no computers, no papers, no lab equipment, no nothing. Just an empty room.

"Oh, come on!" Brooklynn said, frustrated.

Yasmina flipped a light switch, but nothing happened. "If there's no power, how are those cold-air vents running?" she asked.

"And who took everything?" Sammy wondered.

"Something's gotta be here," Brooklynn said. "It's gotta be!"

Brooklynn turned around, running from the

room and down a hallway. Sammy and Yasmina followed. None of them noticed that the front door of the genetics lab was still open . . . or that a snout was slowly entering. . . .

The boys were springing through the jungle and emerged onto a grassy plain. The Stegosaurus was still right behind them, gaining ground.

Just as it was about to strike, WHAM! From out of nowhere, the other Stegosaurus slammed right into it, and the two dinosaurs resumed their fight back in the jungle.

"Okay, that was—" Darius started, only to turn his head and see an enormous, hungry Ceratosaurus right ahead!

CHAPTER TWELVE

There they stood, Kenji clutching his butter knife, feeling exceptionally lame. They waited for the Ceratosaurus to make a move, but instead, it just stood there. Until it . . . walked away?

Darius tilted his head as he watched the Ceratosaurus move toward a large body of water. He had been so concerned with the Stegosauruses that he hadn't even noticed it! The Ceratosaurus reached the water, then bent over, taking a long drink.

And the Ceratosaurus wasn't the only one. Surrounding the water were Stegosauruses, Brachiosauruses, Ankylosauruses, and Parasaurolophuses, all drinking side by side in peace.

"A watering hole!" Darius exclaimed. "Dr. Grant theorized they could become neutral ground for predators and prey under the right conditions. Now, without any fences or people around . . . Kenji, we might be the first people to ever see something like this!"

As Darius continued to watch, he heard sniffling coming from Kenji's direction. He looked over and saw his friend was actually crying!

"It's just so . . . majestic!" Kenji said, and Darius patted his friend on the shoulder.

"I wish Dr. Grant were here," Darius said. "He'd write the most amazing article about this."

"You don't need that guy," Kenji said. "You got your nerd book."

Darius smiled and took out his notebook. "This? Nah, I'm just messing around."

"If this really is something no one has ever seen, I bet you could make that doctor dork mad jealous that *you* saw it and *he* didn't," Kenji said.

"Wanna stay a little longer?" Darius asked.

"Why not?" Kenji said and nestled against a nearby tree. Darius sat down next to him, staring at his notebook. He proceeded to write FIELD GUIDE on the cover.

The girls had made their way into the main room of the genetics lab, and Brooklynn caught sight of something familiar—a framed picture on a desk.

"Eddie!" she said. "Of course!"

"Who?" Sammy asked, looking at the picture of some goofy, grinning guy standing next to an unhappy Dr. Wu.

"The van-stealing birthday weirdo," Brooklynn said. "Remember?"

They had met Eddie weeks ago when they first stumbled upon the genetics lab. At first, they thought Eddie might help them escape the island. But Eddie was only interested in saving himself. Unfortunately, the murderous Indominus rex had other ideas.

"He mentioned something about 'the other guys,'" Brooklynn continued. "And that no one knew what was 'really going on here.' Could he have also been working for Mantah Corp?"

They searched the room but still turned up nothing.

Except for a loud growl. Yasmina and Brooklynn ducked behind Eddie's desk and peered around the side of it. The source of the growl was a blue Baryonyx stalking into the main lab!

The dinosaur entered the lab, and the girls knew they were going to have to make their move. But before they could do anything, Brooklynn clutched Sammy's and Yasmina's arms. Taped to the underside of the desk was a plain manila envelope with E-750 written on it. As quietly as she could, Brooklynn took it off.

"E seven fifty? I know that number," Brooklynn whispered. "It was on Wu's computer!"

"We gotta move, now!" Yasmina said.

The shuffled away, moving to the next desk over. The Baryonyx sniffed and kept looking.

Then Yasmina darted for a nearby incubator. Brooklynn was next, but she tripped over a metal desk chair, falling. The envelope flew from her hand, papers and a key card spilling out onto the floor.

The Baryonyx took notice and was coming for them.

Brooklynn tried to gather the contents of the envelope, but Sammy pulled her away.

Yasmina shoved the incubator into the path of the Baryonyx, who swatted the machine aside with terrifying ease.

The girls had just managed to exit the main lab when they flung the door closed, right on the Baryonyx's snout.

They took a deep breath, only to feel a jolt of fear as another Baryonyx poked its head from a different door.

CHAPTER THIRTEEN

Brooklynn had no idea how long they had been running. They left the genetics lab and didn't look back, and she was almost certain that the Baryonyxes would catch them.

But . . . they didn't!

At last, they slowed down, looking around the underbrush, listening for signs of the dinosaurs . . . and heard nothing. They had made it! It was a moment for rejoicing, but Yasmina noticed that Brooklynn wasn't smiling.

"What's wrong?" she asked.

"It's just, I was so close to finding . . . something," Brooklynn said. "But I dropped the envelope."

"You mean . . . this?" Sammy said, pulling out the papers and key card that had spilled out of the envelope.

"Sammy! You grabbed it?" Brooklynn said, beaming.

"Of course!" Sammy said. "How else are we gonna solve our—"

"Stone-cold mystery!" the girls said in unison.

Brooklynn looked at the papers and saw a series of numbers. Beneath each number, there were the same four letters repeating in different patterns.

"A bunch of numbers and letters," Brooklynn said. Then she looked at the key card. "And this thing. No answers. Just more questions. Maybe we should check if—"

But Brooklynn was cut off by the roar of a Baryonyx.

They were getting close.

"Or we should go," Brooklynn said, and the girls headed back to camp.

By the time Brooklynn, Yasmina, and Sammy got back to camp, Darius and Kenji were already there. Darius was busy writing in his field guide, while Kenji had just finished taking a shower.

Adjusting the towel on his head, Kenji saw the girls and smiled. "I fixed the water!" he said.

"Yeah . . . with a little help," Darius corrected him.

"And we found this!" Brooklynn said, holding

up the key card she had found in the genetics lab.

"Was that something you were looking for?" Darius asked.

"Kinda!" Brooklynn said.

The tree house had really come together, and with the water back up and running, the camp was starting to feel like some kind of home. As the sun began to set, the kids kicked back and relaxed for the first time in ages.

Kenji had found a music player in the rubble that still worked. He played some music, and Sammy and Brooklynn started dancing. Darius was sitting with Yasmina, who was drawing in his field guide.

"That's great," Darius said, looking at Yasmina's illustration. "Can you make the Parasaurolophus crest a little bigger?"

"How's . . . this?" Yasmina asked, sketching away.

"Perfect!" Darius said. He looked at the completed illustration of the watering hole. It looked just like the real thing!

"Whoa!" Sammy suddenly shouted. "Look at *that*!"

She jumped up, pointing at the sunset through

the trees. An array of colors, purples, pinks, and oranges, lit up the sky. They stood in silence, watching the sun dip lower and lower, until . . . another light flickered.

"Is that . . . ," Yasmina said.

"It looks like—" Brooklynn added.

"A campfire," Sammy finished.

"Guys," Darius said with a grin. "We're not alone."

"Someone got our SOS signal!" Kenji said.

Darius turned to face his friend. "Let's go find them. It's time to go home!"

CHAPTER FOURTEEN

The Camp Cretaceous campers raced through the jungle for hours, climbing the occasional tree to keep track of the campfire in the distance. As they got closer and closer to the campfire, their excitement grew. They wondered who had come to save them. Darius wondered if maybe someone like Dr. Alan Grant himself would come!

But when Darius scampered up a tree to check the distance to the campfire, he couldn't see a thing. "The bonfire!" he called out. "It's gone!"

He slid back down the tree, and the other kids saw the look on Darius's face.

"What if . . . they left?" Sammy said. "What if the people who came to save us gave up, and we missed our chance?"

Sammy's words sat with everyone, and a heaviness weighed on the group. There was a rustling sound in the foliage, and then there came a loud THUMP.

Darius screamed.

The kids drew into a circle, holding their make-shift weapons.

"C-could be a really big Compy, right?" Kenji stuttered.

But no one believed that. A dark shadow fell over the group, and the kids slowly turned to see the silhouette of a prowling Ceratosaurus stalking toward them. The creature roared, and the kids ran.

They tried zigzagging through trees to throw the dinosaur off, but the Ceratosaurus was able to maneuver just fine, making hairpin turns between the trees.

Darius led the kids into a thick section of trees as the group swatted at branches, trying to push their way through. The Ceratosaurus was right behind them, gaining ground with every step. Kenji tripped, and his butter knife flew out of his hand. He collided into Sammy, and the two went down.

Brooklynn turned back and pulled both Sammy and Kenji to their feet just as the Ceratosaurus stopped, a few yards away from them. It opened its fanged mouth, grunting.

The kids backed off, waiting for the worst. Then Brooklynn stepped up, clutching a baseball bat in her hands, screaming, "Okay, come on!" She positioned herself between the kids and the Ceratosaurus and was ready to swing.

Suddenly, an arm shoved Brooklynn behind a log, and two pairs of hands pulled the other kids right next to her!

They watched as a flare was lit, the light momentarily blinding them. Then the flare shot across the sky, and the sound of gunfire filled their ears. A burly, stern-looking man with a scar on his cheek came into view, holding a rifle, firing it up into the air. The noise scared off the Ceratosaurus, who turned tail and ran.

Then a man and a woman wearing safari gear and carrying cameras around their necks walked toward the kids. They looked concerned as they approached.

"Oh, thank goodness you're okay!" the woman said.

"You are okay, aren't you?" the man asked.

"Who are you?" Darius said.

"Well, after all that, maybe you should call us your salvation," the woman said as the man reached out a hand to Darius.

Darius took the hand, relieved.

"We don't even know your names," Darius said as he trekked through the jungle with the three newcomers.

"I'm Mitch," the man said. "And my better half here is Tiff. We're ecotourists."

"That's a fancy way of saying we travel to exotic places and photograph rare animals," Tiff explained.

"When we heard what happened here, we were like—"

"Gotta get down here!" Tiff said, finishing Mitch's sentence. "I was fine taking snaps of lions and tigers, but—"

"Pics of dinosaurs in the wild?" Mitch said. "You don't pass that up! Do you, babe?"

"I guess ya don't, babe!" Tiff replied, and Sammy laughed.

"When we activated the emergency distress beacon, we hoped someone would get our signal," Darius said. "I kinda can't believe it worked."

"Oh yes, the signal!" Tiff said, a little too enthusiastically. "Honey, remember when we got that? It was right after the boat dropped us off!"

Darius heard the word "boat," and his heart

soared. Maybe the boat could get them off the island!

A loud THWACK came from ahead, like a blade slicing through plants. Which is exactly what it was. Darius saw the burly guy with the scar on his cheek hacking away with a machete.

"That's our tour guide, Hap," Mitch said. "Came highly recommended. Knows cameras and the outdoors like the back of his hand, but not much of a talker, though."

Hap looked at Mitch, grunted, and went back to clearing the brush.

"Our camp's not much," Mitch continued, "but hopefully you'll be okay roughing it with us."

As they approached the campsite, Darius's jaw nearly hit the ground.

"Is this a dream?" Brooklynn said, her eyes nearly popping out of her skull.

Darius gazed at Mitch and Tiff's campsite in wonder. If this was their idea of "roughing it," he wondered what they were used to! The campsite was more of a glampsite—there was a row of yurts with a generous amount of space between each. The door to one yurt was open, and Darius looked inside to see a large bed with blankets—real blankets! There was even a recliner and a bookshelf inside.

Darius turned to see an outdoor dining area, featuring a large table with all kinds of cookware and place settings. Little lights had been strung up around the site, twinkling in the air around them.

"My goodness," Tiff said with a smile. "I can't imagine how hungry you all must be. Would you like some breakfast?"

Tiff didn't need to ask. The kids were starving, and they all-too-happily sat down at the large table, feasting on the food that Tiff and Mitch offered. They had eggs and biscuits, and there was fresh fruit, and real butter, and juice, and coffee (which Darius's mother said he shouldn't drink because it might stunt his growth, but he had some anyway).

"You're with us now, and you're safe," Mitch said as he watched the kids scarf down their meal. "And when our boat comes back in a couple o' days—"

"After it refuels in Papagayo," Tiff said.

"After it refuels in Papagayo, we'll get you back to the mainland!"

"We're leaving in two days?" Darius said in disbelief.

"Is this really happening?" Sammy said.

"It is, sweetie," Tiff replied. "You're going *home.*"

The kids let out a collective cheer and then kept on eating.

Mitch sat down next to Darius and removed the camera from his neck. Showing it to Darius, he said, "You wanna see some pics we took of Big Five animals in Botswana?"

Turning on the camera, Mitch held the camera out for Darius to see. There were amazing, crystal clear, close-up pictures of an elephant. Then a roaring lion.

"Whoa! These are so cool!" Darius exclaimed. "Got any dinosaur shots?"

"Unfortunately, not yet," Mitch said with a sigh. "Personally, I had my sights on the T. rex. I can't wait to see its craniofacial biting behavior in action. Uh, sorry. I can be a bit of a nerd about dinosaurs."

"Craniofacial talk? I'll *bite*!" Darius said, cringing as the eyes of his friends rolled. "Sorry, that was terrible."

"Looks like we both need *muzzles,*" Mitch said, playing with Darius, and the two burst into laughter.

CHAPTER FIFTEEN

"You, uh, do this for a living, yeah?" Brooklynn asked. She was sitting across from Hap, who hadn't said a word since they sat down to eat. "Not sure if you heard, but I travel the world, too. Yep. Vlogger. Kind of a big deal."

Hap sniffed.

"Okay, so, uh, where have you been, nature guide?"

"Nature places," Hap said, speaking at last.

"Do you take people on photography eco-tours a lot? Mitch said you came highly recommended. Is this your first time working with M—"

Before she could finish, Hap slammed his fork down on the table and glowered at Brooklynn. "No more questions." Then he broke into a smile that chilled Brooklynn. "Your food will get cold."

Tiff stood, clapping her hands. "All right,"

she said loudly, with enough joyful enthusiasm to gloss over the incident. "Why don't you kids freshen up while we clear the table? It's a little primitive—sorry—but in the bathroom yurt you'll find a solar-powered shower and a heated toilet."

The kids got up from the table and headed toward the bathroom yurt. But as Brooklynn stood up, something fell from her pocket.

The key card.

She reached for it, only to find Hap snatching it off the ground first.

"Hey!" Brooklynn said. "That's mine! Give it back!"

Hap looked at the card, completely ignoring Brooklynn. He turned it over, and at last, Brooklynn snatched it back.

She walked away, joining the others at the bathroom yurt, but glanced over her shoulder.

Hap was staring at her.

The butter knife sat in the dirt, and a silent figure glanced at it as he walked past. He took a few more steps and pushed aside a stand of bushes. He lightly ran his hand along the head of the small but sturdy dinosaur next to him. Not too far off, there were harsh voices.

"Where are the kids?" a man in expensive safari clothes asked.

A woman, also in safari clothes, turned and stared sternly at him. She wasn't angry, but she didn't seem completely happy with him either.

Another man, much gruffer, answered, "Still in the bathroom yurt. The chatty internet one is getting suspicious."

The woman and her tough-looking companion traded a guarded look.

"Hap, buddy, relax, the man said, easily blowing off the other man's concern. "We have a plan, and we'll fill ya in later. Let's just go back before they realize we're gone."

As the three adults walked out of view, the figure hiding in the jungle turned to look at his dinosaur companion.

"New plan," he said with a look of calm determination. "Save our friends."

CHAPTER SIXTEEN

The kids crowded into the bathroom yurt, not sure whether they should brush their teeth with the pre-pasted toothbrushes, wash their hands, use one of four different kinds of hand cream, or take a hot shower.

They talked excitedly, but Brooklynn shushed them. "I can't prove it yet," she said. "But I think there's something going on with Hap. He dodged all my questions and was really *weird* about the key card I found in Wu's lab."

Everyone looked at Brooklynn like they just didn't get it.

"Mitch and Tiff are clueless," Brooklynn said dismissively. "She's too 'Golly, goodness' to notice anything, and all *he* thinks about is dinosaurs."

"What's wrong with that?" Darius asked.

"I'm just saying Hap's suspicious." Brooklynn

grumbled. "He's gruff and unsmiling and—"

Yasmina raised an eyebrow. "What's wrong with that?"

"Look," Brooklynn said, exasperated. "Could Hap be involved with Mantah Corp?"

Sammy looked at Brooklynn. "I mean, the Mantah Corp folks who sent me were like *corporate* spies, not . . . action-man, secret-identity, *pew-pew* spies."

"I know you've got conspiracy stuff on the brain, Brooklynn," Darius said. "But forget Hap. In two days, we're going home. Let's focus on that."

Sammy nodded. "Don't worry, Brooklynn. Just in case, we'll keep our eyes open."

After they emerged from the bathroom yurt, Brooklynn caught a glimpse of Hap hauling two large duffel bags. As quietly as she could, she followed Hap as he approached the row of yurts. Brooklynn stopped at the last one and slowly peered around the corner.

Somehow, Hap was gone!

Then she felt a hand on her shoulder. . . .

"What are you doing?"

Darius flashes back to when he and the other Camp Cretaceous survivors were so close to getting off the island . . .

. . . and to the moment they lost Ben.

Darius realizes that there's an emergency beacon that can be activated to call for help.

Unfortunately, the emergency beacon has become part of the T. rex's nest on Main Street.

The T. rex does not like anything—or anyone—invading her territory.

Armed with a pair of kids' walkie-talkies, Darius and Kenji plan to sneak into the T. rex's nest to activate the beacon . . .

. . . while Yasmina and Brooklynn keep an eye out for the dinosaur.

The kids don't know if they succeeded, but they feel good about working as a team . . .

. . . and as usual, they end up on the run. Sammy and Brooklyn help the injured Yasmina.

The kids confront the angry Carnotaurus they nicknamed Toro . . .

. . . and Toro is not going to forget them.

Jurassic World is filled with beauty and wonder . . .

. . . but so much danger, too.

As the dinosaurs reclaim more and more of the island for their own . . .

. . . the kids feel like they are never going to get off the island. Will help ever arrive?

Brooklynn jumped, only to see Kenji standing there. He had a mischievous grin on his face.

"Is it spying?" Kenji asked.

"No! It is *not* spying!" Brooklynn said. "Okay, it *is* spying. What are *you* doing?"

"Dude, I just had to get away from Tiff and Mitch. I don't get how anyone can stand them! It's like, we get it. You're rich. You don't have to throw it in our faces."

Brooklynn stared at Kenji as if to say, "Dude, that's *you*!"

Suddenly, they heard Hap muttering. Kenji and Brooklynn leaned around the edge of the yurt and saw Hap walking toward a yurt, holding some cameras. He fumbled with one, trying to take it apart, but it was clear he had no idea what he was doing.

"Nope, not at all weird that a guide for *photographers* isn't good with cameras," Brooklynn whispered.

Hap shook one of the cameras in frustration, nearly dropping it. He raised his lip into a sneer and left the cameras on the ground, picking up the duffel bags instead and heading inside the yurt. The kids could see a faint flicker of blue light coming from inside.

"We gotta get into that yurt," Brooklynn said.

"Look!" Mitch said.

Darius walked over to the ecotourist standing alone at the edge of the camp, behind a tree. Mitch had a finger to his lips as he motioned to Darius. A familiar chittering sound could be heard, and Darius knew immediately that it was a group of Compsognathuses.

"Awww, so cute!" Tiff said loudly, barging in. "Come here, little guy!"

"No, stop!" Darius said.

Tiff ran over to a Compy, trying to pet it. Darius, Mitch, and the other kids who had joined Tiff were horrified!

The Compy turned toward Tiff, hissing. The other Compys started to hiss, too, and they looked like they were ready to pounce on the ecotourist.

Tiff screamed.

"Hey!" Darius shouted toward the Compys. "Over here!"

The Compys swiveled their heads to look in Darius's direction. He was holding a granola bar that he had swiped from the breakfast table. Waving it in front of the dinosaurs, Darius then tossed it into some nearby bushes.

The Compys took the bait and chased after the granola bar, Tiff forgotten.

"That was close," Darius said. "They look cute, but they actually have trace amounts—"

"Of venom in their bites," Mitch said, admiringly. "Quick thinking, D! How did you know that would work?"

Darius smiled and pulled out his field guide. "I've been keeping a log of their scavenging. And other dinosaur behaviors," he said. "I mean, it's not much. . . ."

Mitch took the guide in his hands and flipped through, Tiff looking over his shoulder. "This is incredible, Darius!"

"And Yaz drew all the pictures," Darius added. "Pretty great, right?"

Mitch and Tiff kept flipping through the field guide, and Darius watched as their expressions changed and their faces seemed to fall.

"We haven't seen a tenth of the dinosaurs you have," Tiff said. "Maybe we've been looking in the wrong places?"

"We've only got two days to see these magnificent animals," Mitch said. "When the legal battles end and this park closes for good, what will all this have been for? Will it still mean anything to anyone?"

Darius looked at the ecotourists and then back at the Compys, who were still foraging for the granola bar. He had been so consumed with survival and trying to be rescued. Now that the rescue was nearly here, it finally dawned on him that he was going to be leaving Jurassic World. Forever. He might never see another living dinosaur again.

"Hey, two days is still plenty of time to explore," Darius said, brightening. "In fact, I know a place not too far from here that will blow your minds. You in?"

Tiff and Mitch nodded, smiling at Darius.

Suddenly, an alarm blared, and the Compys scattered.

CHAPTER SEVENTEEN

Kenji and Brooklynn covered their ears, trying to block out the sound of the alarm.

"You!"

Brooklynn whirled around, only to see Hap staring at her.

"Stay away from the yurt!" Hap demanded.

All she had done was touch the yurt—she hadn't even opened the door yet—and the alarm sounded.

"What's going on?" Tiff said, racing up behind Hap as Mitch and the other kids followed.

Hap grumbled and pulled out a key fob. Pressing a button, the alarm shut off. He pointed at Brooklynn and Kenji and said, "Isn't it obvious? The chatty one was trying to sneak into the yurt. These kids can't go snooping into private spaces!"

Brooklynn glared at Hap, who glared right

back at her. *What is his deal?*

"Now, now, Hap," Tiff said. "I'm sure it was all a misunderstanding."

"Misunderstanding?!" Hap said, not buying it.

Then he took a step toward Brooklynn and leaned in. "Do yourself a favor . . . and stay out of my yurt!"

"Let's talk about this calmly, 'kay?" Tiff said, grabbing Hap's arm. She led him away from the group as she turned and gave the kids a forced smile as if to say, "Sorry!"

"Sorry about that," Mitch said, moving the kids away from the yurt. "It's our first time working with Hap, and he's very protective of his yurt. Set it up himself, moved all the equipment in. Hasn't even allowed us in."

"Ha!" Brooklynn said. "See? See?"

"Maybe we should postpone our trek. You've all been through a lot," Mitch said, turning to look at Brooklynn. "Especially *that one,* it seems."

"No, it's fine," Darius said. "Brooklynn won't touch the yurt, and we'll all go to the place I wanted to show you."

Brooklynn stared at Darius, gritting her teeth. "Uh, Darius? I think maybe we should freshen up before we decide that."

"We already freshened up," Darius said.

"Can never be too fresh!" Brooklynn insisted.

Inexplicably, they were back inside the bathroom yurt, huddled around the toilet.

"Really?" Yasmina said. "There isn't *anywhere* else we can talk?'

"Hap is hiding something!" Brooklynn said. "Why put an alarm on a yurt?"

"Uh . . . so a dinosaur or a *you* can't sneak in and wreck his stuff?" Yasmina offered.

Darius threw his hands up. "You can't just let this conspiracy stuff go, huh?" he said. "And for what? A new video to boost your followers?"

"Who said anything about followers?" Brooklynn snapped. "You think I'm doing this to get attention?"

"Yes! That's your whole deal!'

"And what's your whole deal, Darius? Dinosaurs? You care more about them than actual people!"

"That's hilarious, *you* calling *me* selfish."

Brooklynn's eyes sharpened. "You're obsessed. Just because Mitch is acting all 'cool dad' with you doesn't—"

At the mention of the word "dad," Darius's expression changed completely. It was like the life drained out of him. Instantly, Brooklynn realized what she had said. Darius had lost his father, and she hadn't meant to tear at that still-open wound.

"Oh no, Darius, I d-didn't . . . ," she said, reaching out to him.

But Darius wasn't listening. He turned around and exited the bathroom yurt.

The other kids followed, leaving Brooklynn behind.

CHAPTER EIGHTEEN

"Aren't you going to go with them?"

Brooklynn was at the edge of the camp, watching Darius take off with Sammy, Yasmina, Mitch, and Tiff on their dinosaur-photographing expedition. She was trying to fight off the tears that had come from upsetting her friend.

"No, I'm staying here," Kenji said. Then he smiled at Brooklynn. "I know you didn't mean the 'dad' thing. It was a slip. Happens to everyone. Even me. Especially me. Look, Darius knows you didn't mean it that way, too. Just give him time."

Brooklynn looked at Kenji, and suddenly, her whole demeanor changed. "Come on," she said. "Even if Hap reset the alarm, I can disarm it."

She turned around and headed back into camp.

"Wait, what?!" Kenji said, watching his friend approach Hap's yurt.

"Okay, how did 'give him time' turn into 'break back into the yurt'?" Kenji asked.

"Because once I prove I'm right, Darius will *have* to forgive me," she said.

"I can't believe *I'm* the voice of reason here," Kenji said with a sigh. "Brooklynn—"

Before they could take another step, they heard someone clearing their throat. Turning on their heels, they saw Hap, waiting by the yurt.

"Mitch and Tiff asked me to go with them," Hap said slowly. "But I said, nah . . . I'll make sure *those two* don't get into any trouble. Let's not make this any more unpleasant than it needs to be."

Hap placed his large hands on the kids' shoulders and promptly guided them away from his yurt.

"You guys are gonna love this place!" Darius said, bounding up the grassy hill. "It's just up here!"

When they reached the top of the hill, Darius pointed to the valley below. There was a herd of Brachiosauruses grazing. Mitch and Tiff stared at the placid scene, their jaws open.

"Wow," Mitch said.

Darius looked at Mitch, then gave him a sly smile. Cupping his hands over his mouth, Darius let out a Brachiosaurus call. Then another.

Mitch cupped his hands around his mouth and imitated Darius.

Then the Brachiosauruses bellowed back!

Mitch looked at the dinosaurs with awe and wonder.

Darius pulled out his field guide, flipping through its pages. "If you think this is cool, there is one more place we could go."

"The watering hole?" Mitch said, looking at the page in Darius's field guide.

"Just my favorite place on the island!" Darius said. "I mean, getting that close to so many herbivores and carnivores? And nobody's fighting?"

Mitch and Tiff looked at one another, clearly interested.

"You could get lots of good pictures there!" Sammy said. "There's *so* many dinosaurs!"

"Babe, what would we do without this kid?" Mitch said, squeezing Darius's arm softly.

"Let me radio Hap with the change of plans," Tiff said. "It's watering hole day!"

Darius smiled. For the first time in what seemed like forever, he was truly happy.

"Come in, Hap! Hap, come in!"

Tiff's voice crackled over the walkie-talkie, unheard by both Kenji and Brooklynn, who had fallen asleep at the dining table.

Hap picked up the walkie-talkie and walked away from the sleeping kids.

The moment he was out of sight, Brooklynn's eyes snapped open. She had only been faking sleep. Then she nudged Kenji, who actually *had* fallen asleep.

"Come on," Brooklynn said. "Now's our chance."

They ran quietly over to the row of yurts and were just about to go inside Hap's tent.

"No, you listen!"

It was Hap, on the walkie-talkie! He was just a few feet away, pacing by the yurt. The kids ducked for cover and listened.

"I'm done!" Hap continued. "No, this isn't a threat. This is a *promise.* Stay out of my way. I'll take care of these kids *myself.*"

They watched as Hap ducked into his yurt. When he reemerged, he was carrying an Asset Containment Unit stun spear in one hand.

Brooklynn and Kenji were off and running.

CHAPTER NINETEEN

"Babe, you okay?" Mitch asked.

Tiff had hurried back to the group, but all the color had drained from her face. "Ya know, babe, I think we should pack up, head back to camp."

"Uh, what's going on?" Yasmina asked.

Tiff looked at Mitch, hesitating. "Oh, nothing big," she said haltingly. "Just an . . . odd conversation with Hap. Why don't we go? Now. Okay? Okay!"

Mitch nodded and started to run back down the hill.

"Do you think . . . ?" Sammy said softly, exchanging worried looks with Yasmina.

"I'm sure everything's fine," Darius said.

But when they arrived back at Mitch and Tiff's

glampsite, there was no sign of Brooklynn or Kenji.

"Guys!" Yasmina shouted.

"Brooklynn?" Sammy called out.

"He's not in the bathroom, either!" Tiff said. "Children, Mitchell and I are going to have a quick grown-up conference. You stay put. We'll brb, 'kay?"

Then Mitch grabbed Tiff, pulling her aside. Darius watched as they spoke to one another rapidly, the exchange becoming heated.

In that moment, Darius knew that Brooklynn had been right.

Brooklynn and Kenji were sprinting through the jungle, trying to put as much distance between themselves and Hap and that stun spear as they possibly could.

The kids could hear the rustling sound of brush being pushed aside and knew it was Hap, hot on their heels.

"Keep . . . going!" Brooklynn said, panting.

They poured on the speed, moving even faster. They made it through the jungle and into a clearing. There was foliage all around them. Before they could take another step and duck back into the jungle, the kids heard a voice.

"I told you to stay put."

Suddenly, Hap jumped from the bushes, blocking their path with the stun spear.

"You have no idea who you're dealing with," Hap said.

But before he could finish, Brooklynn and Kenji flinched in horror as something darted from the bushes. Something fast. It attacked Hap, swinging what looked like a thick tree branch or a walking stick. The tree branch connected, and Hap tumbled to the ground.

Kenji and Brooklynn looked up, and at last got a good look at the person who had saved them.

"Ben?!" Kenji said.

CHAPTER TWENTY

"Wait, explain this again?" an astonished Brooklynn said.

Ben stood before her and Kenji, along with his now much bigger dinosaur, Bumpy, but it still wasn't registering. *Ben really was alive!*

Brooklynn couldn't take her eyes off Ben. Just the sight of him was overwhelming, completely unreal. She thought for sure that Ben had lost his life in the fall from the train. They all had. And now there he was, alive as could be.

While Brooklynn and Kenji could barely contain their excitement at seeing their lost friend alive, Ben seemed to be completely nonchalant. He shrugged as he tied Hap up with vines. Neither Brooklynn nor Kenji said anything, but the looks on their faces practically screamed "How the heck did you survive that fall, and how are you even here?"

Ben looked at his friends and saw the disbelief on their faces. Wearily, like it was already an old story, he said, "Fell off monorail. Got savaged by Pteranodons. Plummeted into a lake. Crawled out of the lake. Lost Bumpy. Found Bumpy. Overheard that couple say they were going to leave you all here to die." He paused for a moment as though he were trying to remember something that wasn't really all that important. "And I defeated Toro. Oh, and I may be immortal. Too soon to tell."

Kenji stared at Ben, trying to take it all in. Ben had just blown through what sounded like an astonishing series of events and made it all seem like it was no big deal. He'd survived the Pteranodons . . . the part about defeating Toro! That Carnotaurus had given the kids so much trouble during their initial attempt to escape the island. The creature had them cornered and had nearly eaten Darius! And now here was Ben, saying that he had single-handedly defeated the dinosaur! Kenji tried to act cool, but he was impressed. The germaphobe had survived.

And more than that, it was apparent that in the weeks that Ben had been separated from his friends, he had become like a new person. Gone was the Ben who always looked like he was going to throw up and was constantly slathering his hands in sanitizer. In his place was a new Ben. This new Ben was steely eyed and carried a big stick. He looked like he was born in the jungle and exuded a calm fearlessness.

Finished with the vines, Ben looked at Hap's stun spear on the ground, picking it up. He twirled it around, then stuck it in his belt in one motion. The spear reminded him a little of the one that he had fashioned for himself out of a long stick and a rock—the same one he used to face Toro.

Then he spit.

"New Ben is metal," Brooklynn said.

"Who cares! He's back!" Kenji said, throwing his arms around Ben.

Ben went in for the hug but then surprised Kenji by unfastening his fanny pack, the one that Kenji had been carrying around since Ben disappeared.

"We've got bigger grubs to fry," Ben said. "Like figuring out what to do with Hap. I say we feed him to the Mosasaurus. Or the T. rex. Or—"

"Or you could listen to me," Hap said.

Everyone jumped as they saw Hap sit up.

"You're awake?" Brooklynn asked.

"Of course I'm awake," Hap said. "You can't actually knock someone out by just hitting them on the head. You kids have to trust me. I'm trying to save your lives!"

"Uh, what's going on?" Darius asked as he watched Mitch and Tiff pulling out boxes and duffel bags. "Do we really need all this to go look for Brooklynn, Kenji, and Hap?"

Mitch and Tiff exchanged looks; then Mitch smiled at the kids. "Just wanna be prepared for whatever we might encounter along the way. After all, the boat'll be here in three days. You wanna be rescued in one piece, don't you?"

"You said the boat would be here in *two* days," Yasmina corrected.

Mitch waved. "Two to three days. Right, babe?"

"Hundred percent," Tiff said. "Now grab that *stuff* we need from Hap's tent."

Sammy watched as Mitch headed into a yurt . . . that wasn't Hap's. "Um, I thought you said *that* one was Hap's?"

"Why don't you kids have some chocolate?" Tiff said, cutting her off. "It's from France! And over there!"

Before anyone could protest, Tiff shoved them into the dining area.

"I can't be the only one who thought that was weird," Yasmina said quietly. "How do you forget what day the boat is coming back?"

"And they're being kinda shady about all that stuff they're packing," Sammy added.

"And about that tent," Darius said, gesturing at the yurt.

The three kids looked at each other, and almost at once, an unspoken plan began to form in their minds.

CHAPTER TWENTY-ONE

"What's in that?" Sammy said, pointing at a bag of gear that Mitch and Tiff had gathered.

"Huh?" Tiff said.

"Oh, what's in that?" Sammy continued, pointing at another bag. Turning to Mitch, she said, "Favorite color, favorite food, favorite color of food—go!"

"I . . . What?" Mitch said.

While Sammy distracted Mitch and Tiff, Darius snuck into the mysterious yurt. Once inside, he saw a folding table. Something was sitting on top of it, under a tarp. Darius noticed that there were all kinds of traps on the ground, like ones that might be used to capture wild animals . . . or dinosaurs. And leaning up against a wall were hunting rifles and ACU stun spears.

"What . . . ?" Darius muttered as he approached the tarp on the table. Lifting it aside, he saw the horns of a Sinoceratops underneath.

Darius gasped and backed away . . . right . . . into . . . Mitch.

"Whatcha doing in here, D?" Mitch asked with an ominous grin.

"How, exactly, is chasing us through the jungle saving our lives?" Brooklynn asked. "*Plus,* we heard you tell Mitch and Tiff you were going to 'take care' of us."

"I'm trying to!" Hap said, looking at the vines knotted rather lamely around his wrists. "By getting you *home.* I was gonna take you somewhere safe and then force Mitch and Tiff to sail us *all* to Costa Rica."

Then Hap shot an icy look at Ben. "But then you ran off. Feral boy and his dino pal showed up. And everything went sideways."

At the mention of "feral boy," Ben raised his head to glare at Hap. His lips curled into a smile, and he grunted in approval.

Hap turned to face Brooklynn.

"We have a boat moored at the northwest dock," he said.

"There's a way off the island?" Kenji said in disbelief.

"You all said it was refueling—" Brooklynn pointed out.

Rolling his eyes, Hap said, "Yeah, they lied."

"Wow, *that's* supposed to make us believe you?" Brooklynn argued.

"Listen! I scouted out some kind of garage near here when we first landed. We can take a vehicle, get to the dock, and *prove* I'm telling the truth. But only if you untie me."

Brooklynn just stared at Hap as if to say, "Yeah, like *that's* ever gonna happen."

"Look, I'm no angel," Hap said. "I was paid to kill dinos. But Mitch and Tiff, they're *nuts*. I'm not about to leave a bunch of kids here to die."

As Hap stood waiting for an answer, Brooklynn conferred with Ben and Kenji. "Is he telling the truth about a garage?" she whispered.

"I don't know," Kenji said. "Maybe?"

"He's lying," Ben said. "I can smell it on him."

In the weeks that Ben had survived alone in the dinosaur-filled jungle, he had smelled stuff that he never would have before. A ton of dinosaur dung, for starters. And grubs, which had a real particular smell that he no longer entirely hated—especially because he loved the taste. (You couldn't be picky about things like that when you were trying to survive.) So it didn't exactly surprise Brooklynn and Kenji when Ben said that he could smell Hap lying.

"If he's telling the truth, Darius, Sammy, and Yaz are in big trouble," Kenji replied. "We have to trust him."

"You're not ecotourists," Darius said. "You're—"

Mitch smiled, holding an ACU tablet. "Big-game hunters, yeah," he said. "Honestly, I'm glad you've seen this, Darius. Friends shouldn't lie to each other."

"You said you got our distress beacon!"

"Oh yeah, *no* idea what that is. But we didn't want you to start asking questions. And hey, it all ended up working out. Bought this ACU tablet. It was supposed to help us track the dinos, but—"

"The grid's down," Darius said.

"Uh-huh. And despite Hap coming highly recommended, he's been pretty useless at finding dinos. He doesn't know half the stuff about them—or the island—that you do. So now *you* can help us!"

"How could you possibly think I'd help you kill dinosaurs? I thought you cared about them!"

"I do," Mitch said, a look of wonder crossing his face. "I've been waiting my whole life for this. Living, breathing dinosaurs up close and personal? But Isla Nublar is under quarantine. The dinosaurs, they've been abandoned. Forgotten. We're the last people to *ever* see them. I'm trying to preserve the memory of Jurassic World."

Darius looked at Mitch sadly.

"Don't you get it?" Mitch said, his voice rising. "Thanks to us, these magnificent creatures will live on forever!"

"By mounting their heads on your wall!" Darius protested.

The smile fell away from Mitch's face as he grabbed Darius, shoving him toward the exit. "I'm disappointed. I really thought we understood each other, D. But I'll make this easy for you."

Mitch and Darius stepped outside the yurt, where Tiff was standing behind Sammy and Yasmina.

"You help us bag the dinosaurs we want, and we'll take you and your friends home. You don't . . . and we leave you all here. Abandoned and forgotten, just like the dinos."

Mitch leaned down, looking Darius in the eyes. Then he smiled. "So, Darius? What's it gonna be?"

CHAPTER TWENTY-TWO

"Well, at least *she* knows how to tie a knot," Hap said.

Brooklynn, Kenji, and Ben were trekking through the jungle toward the garage, with Hap in tow. Brooklynn had retied the vines around Hap, and Ben was leading the big-game hunter with another vine tied to him like a leash.

"I'm telling you, he's leading us into a trap," Ben said.

Ben handed the leash off to Brooklynn as he went ahead to wrangle Bumpy. Kenji walked onward, wondering if Ben was right. After all, the kid had survived for weeks out in the jungle alone. And if he could do that then maybe he knew what he was talking about with Hap, too.

"You hate this, don't you?" Hap said with a certain grim pleasure. "Not knowing the truth. Not knowing if you can trust me."

"Because you've done such a bang-up job acting trustworthy," Brooklynn jabbed.

"Serves me right," Hap said. "Couldn't make up my mind what to do with *you* either, until it was too late. Your pals were ready to swallow lies, but *you* needed to know the truth. Even if it puts you at odds with everyone."

Brooklynn whirled around. "*You* don't know anything about me!"

"Of course I do. You're like me," Hap said. "Unrelenting, suspicious . . . and able to make the hard calls 'cause of it. I'm asking you to make a hard call now. I am not your enemy."

Brooklynn stared at Hap, taking a long, deep breath. She couldn't read his face, and it made her angry.

"Brooklynn, look!"

She turned at the sound of Kenji's voice and went up ahead. With Hap in tow, Brooklynn stepped through some foliage and saw a large garage.

"Believe me now?" Hap said.

Just as the kids and Hap approached the garage in search of a vehicle, Bumpy dug in her heels. She started to bellow loudly.

There was a brief moment of silence, followed by loud barking from the jungle . . . as three Baryonyxes emerged.

"This is bad," Brooklynn whispered.

"This is great!" Mitch said. "I know it wasn't easy, but you made the right choice. Thanks to you, we'll be done in no time!"

Darius was leading the group through the-jungle, clutching his field guide. Sammy and Yasmina walked with him as Mitch followed behind with a stun spear. He and Tiff were lugging big duffel bags full of gear, as well as a weapons bag.

Tiff grimaced as she slapped at a mosquito. "I never wanted kids, and now we've got three of them. And no guide!"

"We don't need a guide, babe," Mitch said. "We have Darius. And he's taking us to, drumroll please . . ."

"The watering hole," Darius said glumly.

"A one-stop dino-hunting shop!" Mitch hollered. "This kid is something. Didn't I tell you this kid is something, Tiff?"

Darius looked like he was drowning. He was the one who had mentioned the watering hole to Mitch. So everything that was about to happen? That was his fault.

Sammy and Yasmina looked at each other in concern. Then Sammy glanced down at Yasmina's injured ankle and blinked.

Picking up on Sammy's meaning, Yasmina stopped walking, grabbing at her ankle. Tiff nearly ran into her.

"What?" Tiff said, exasperated.

"Ankle hurts. I need a break," Yasmina said.

"Fine," Tiff said, swatting away another mosquito. Mitch grabbed her gear while she kept on smacking her hand at the bugs.

"We can't just go along with this," Yasmina whispered to Darius. "We have to do something!"

"We only have two choices," Darius said. "Help them and get back to our families, or don't, and stay trapped here."

"It's locked!" Kenji said, frantically pulling on the handle of one of the garage doors.

The Baryonyxes were getting closer. They hadn't seen the kids or Hap yet, but they were getting closer.

Trying to evade the dinosaurs, Brooklynn bumped up against the scanner next to the door. Suddenly, there was a soft BEEP as the door opened! At once, it dawned on Brooklynn, and she pulled out the key card she had found in Dr. Wu's lab, smiling.

"Go-go-go!" Ben said as they dashed inside the garage, closing the door softly behind them.

Inside, all they could see were tires, crates, and gas cans. There were no big vehicles, but there was a motorcycle with a side car.

"It's a master key!" Brooklynn said, staring at the key card. "It could open something in Wu's lab. It could open everything!"

Hap turned to look at Kenji and Ben, confused. "What's she talking about?"

Looking around, Brooklynn spotted another scanner near a small door. She pulled on the knob. It wouldn't turn. So she waved the key card in front of the pad. The small door still wouldn't open.

But a pair of large garage doors on the other side of the room did.

And as they slowly crept upward, Brooklynn saw the three Baryonyxes standing there. The creatures turned their heads, looking at the group.

Then they ran.

"Shut the door!" Kenji shouted as Bumpy brayed loudly.

Brooklynn swiped the key card over the pad, but the door just kept on opening.

"How do we get out of here?" Ben shouted.

CHAPTER TWENTY-THREE

The motorcycle roared out of the garage, leaving the three Baryonyxes very confused. Brooklynn was driving the motorcycle, while Kenji sat behind her, holding the stun spear. Hap, still tied up, was in the sidecar. Ben was riding Bumpy next to them.

Unfortunately, the Baryonyxes had not remained confused for long. They quickly gave chase and were gaining.

"Untie me," Hap shouted. "I can help!"

Brooklynn turned her head to look at Hap, then over her shoulder. The Baryonyxes were even closer now.

"Trust me," Hap said.

"Kenji—do it!" Brooklynn ordered.

"You're sure? Like, *sure* sure?" Kenji asked.

Brooklynn nodded. Without another word, Kenji tugged a knot in the vine, releasing Hap. The hunter grabbed the stun spear from Kenji and stood up in the sidecar.

"We all make mistakes, right, kid?" Hap said. "I'm making up for mine right now. You kids . . . live a good, long life."

Before Brooklynn could do anything, Hap unclamped the sidecar from the motorcycle. The bike raced forward, freed of the extra weight. She watched helplessly as Hap drifted behind, leaping from the sidecar with the stun spear.

Now it was just Hap against the Baryonyxes. They closed in around him as the kids pulled away.

The motorcycle was heading into the grassland at the edge of the jungle. Kenji managed one last look over his shoulder and saw the Baryonyxes leap at Hap.

"Hap," Kenji said. "He . . ."

"He made the hard call," Brooklynn said, forcing back her tears.

The rustling sound grabbed everyone's attention. All at once, Darius was on alert.

Mitch and Tiff crouched down low, grabbing the kids as they ducked behind some foliage. Dropping their bags, Tiff pulled out a rifle and passed it to Mitch, then took one for herself.

Stepping out from the jungle was a grazing Stegosaurus, lumbering slowly.

"Perfect," Tiff said.

"She's beautiful, isn't she?" Mitch agreed.

"Take the shot before it gets away," Tiff urged.

As the "ecotourists" raised their rifles, Darius suddenly had an idea. He flipped through his field guide, stopping on a particular page. He smiled at Yasmina and Sammy, and they nodded.

Mitch was taking aim and already squeezing the trigger when Darius jumped to his feet and whistled.

The Stegosaurus immediately looked up and, seeing Darius, started to charge!

"Look out!" Mitch cried as he and Tiff dove out of the way. Sammy and Yasmina grabbed Darius, yanking him to safety just as the Stegosaurus thundered their way, stomping on a duffel bag.

"You!" Mitch screamed, staring at Darius.

The Stegosaurus slammed its tail on the ground, right between Mitch and Tiff.

The kids raced off, Darius still clutching the field guide in his hand.

The Stegosaurus was behind them, and Darius took a deep breath—just as Tiff and Mitch jumped out from behind the brush. Mitch snagged Darius with a free hand, while Tiff threw her weapons bag at Sammy, knocking her to the ground.

Tiff lashed out, her hand catching Yasmina.

Mitch dragged Darius over to the other kids, but Darius pretended to stumble. In that moment, he tore a page from his field guide and shoved it into Yasmina's waiting hand.

Turning, Yasmina rammed her elbow right into Tiff's stomach, causing her to fall to the jungle floor! Yasmina started to run, but Tiff grabbed her bad ankle. Then, from out of nowhere, Sammy tackled Tiff. Yasmina was free!

Yasmina hesitated for a moment, but Sammy shouted, "Go!"

The track star took off, disappearing into the jungle.

Mitch and Tiff glowered at Darius and Sammy.

"I trusted you, Darius," Mitch said. "And you betrayed me! You had a simple choice, and you chose to save dinosaurs over your friends?"

"I didn't," Darius said. "I'm saving us all."

"What the heck is that supposed to mean?" Mitch said.

Tiff sneered and shoved Darius into Sammy. Then she took the stun spear from her partner.

"It doesn't matter," Tiff said. "He's still taking us to the watering hole. Because now, we aren't asking."

Tiff smiled as she activated the stun spear, holding it inches away from Darius and Sammy.

CHAPTER TWENTY-FOUR

Yasmina hadn't sprinted this hard since . . . since before she hurt her ankle. She was running full out, completely ignoring the splint on her leg. As she pounded the ground, her footfalls grew faster and faster, her momentum carrying her along.

She was going so fast that the splint on her ankle cracked, breaking off.

Yasmina skidded around a tree. Her eyes grew wide as she almost collided with Brooklynn and Kenji on their motorcycle!

Brooklynn hit the brakes, and she and Kenji jumped off the motorcycle, allowing it to fall to the ground.

"Yaz!" Kenji cried. "What happened?"

"Where's Sammy and Darius?" Brooklynn asked.

"Tiff and Mitch have them," Yasmina said, panting for air. "They think Darius is leading them to the watering hole so they can kill all the dinosaurs there."

"Darius would never do that," Kenji said.

Yasmina took a series of short breaths and looked at the slip of paper that Darius had shoved into her hand. Opening it up, she saw that it was a map of the Park, with a smudge on one location.

"You're right. He's not taking them to the watering hole. He's leading them there," Yasmina said, pointing to the smudge.

She was pointing at Main Street.

The home of the T. rex.

"Wait, what?!" Brooklynn exclaimed. "He's taking Tiff and Mitch to Main Street?!"

Before Yasmina could say a word, a group of bushes parted, and out popped Ben and Bumpy. Ben nodded and offered his hand for a handshake.

Yasmina stared at him like she was seeing a ghost. Her hand trembled as she held it out to him. As soon as Ben grasped her hand, she let herself be pulled to her feet without taking her eyes off him. Once she was standing, Yasmina threw her arms around Ben and hugged him tight. "You're . . . ," she began. Ben smiled as she continued to squeeze. Despite it all, he was glad to be back, too.

"Yeah, yeah, Ben's alive—we're very happy about it," Brooklynn said impatiently. "But in more pressing news, Darius isn't taking the hunters to the watering hole!"

She showed Ben the page from Darius's journal. "Why would he take them straight to the T. rex?" Ben asked. Something about it just didn't sit right with him.

Kenji's eyes lit up. "Home-court advantage. Darius and Sammy know the terrain, and Tiff and Mitch don't. It'll be easier to lose them on Main Street than in the jungle."

"Then what are we waiting for?" Yasmina said. "Let's go help them!"

The only way the group could get to Darius and Sammy in time would be if they took a shortcut. And the only shortcut available to them was the series of underground maintenance tunnels they had explored weeks ago.

The tunnels were often roamed by not-so-friendly dinosaurs, but thankfully, this trip proved uneventful—until they reached the huge security gate. It wouldn't open.

"It's not budging," said Ben as Bumpy hit the door with her tail. He knew exactly how hard Bumpy could hit, too—the dinosaur had slammed her tail into Toro's ribs during their battle. So if she couldn't make so much as a dent in the door, then it wasn't moving.

Each kid took turns pounding on it, to no avail. If they couldn't get past this gate, then they'd never get to Main Street in time.

A moment later, Ben turned his head to the side. "What is that?"

Brooklynn looked at Ben, and then she heard the noise, too. Squinting her eyes, she looked into the shadows and saw a small door she hadn't noticed before. She walked over and put her ear to the door. There was a humming sound coming from the other side.

Next to the door was a small keypad, and Brooklynn smiled. She waved her key card over the pad, and the door opened with a WHOOSH!

The kids were stunned to enter a tunnel with working lights—electricity! Suddenly, a blast of freezing-cold air hit them.

"Whoa!" Ben said with a shiver. "It's cold enough in here—"

"To freeze flowers," Brooklynn finished.

CHAPTER TWENTY-FIVE

"This isn't the watering hole," Mitch said through gritted teeth. "Does this look like a watering hole, babe?"

Tiff grasped a spear in her hands as the couple advanced on Darius and Sammy, dropping the duffel bags they'd been carrying in the middle of Main Street.

"Sure doesn't, babe," Tiff replied.

"Oh, it's just through this—" Darius started to say.

"Don't lie to me, Darius," Mitch interrupted.

"I swear," Darius said. "I wouldn't *toy* with you."

Sammy raised an eyebrow at the word "toy" and then looked around. They were standing right in front of the gift shop, and there was a shelf full of toys right behind them.

Tiff took a step forward, forcing Sammy and

Darius to take a step back, right into the shelf.

"You little . . . ," Tiff said, snarling. "Do you two think this is some kind of jo—"

"NOW!" Darius shouted.

The kids whipped around, pushing the shelf full of battery-operated dinosaur toys right into Mitch and Tiff. The toys came alive with lights and sounds, startling the "ecotourists." Mitch's weapons bag slid off his shoulder, and Sammy snatched it away. She took off running down Main Street, with Darius right behind her.

In seconds, the kids had disappeared into the shadows.

"The plan . . . actually . . . worked," Sammy said as Darius helped her with the weapons bag.

"Not yet," he said, panting. "We have their guns, but we still gotta lose . . . them."

"Kids! Darius? Come back! We just wanna talk!" Mitch called out.

Darius and Sammy looked at each other, knowing that was probably the *last* thing Mitch wanted. They started to run faster as Darius said, "Split up!"

"Where'd they go?" Tiff growled.

Stopping for a moment, Mitch looked into the darkness, then pointed. "There!"

The couple saw Sammy and Darius take off in different directions. Tiff went after Sammy, while Mitch headed for Darius.

"What is all this?" Yasmina asked, puzzled.

The kids had emerged inside a musty room with low lighting. They could just make out that they were in a command center of some kind. There were large control panels everywhere, along with multiple viewing monitors. None of the equipment was on, but the background hum of electricity was still there.

Kenji looked around and saw a symbol on the wall that he instantly recognized. "Oh, snap! This must be, like, some kinda secret backup power center!"

"We gotta find a way to raise that gate and get to Sammy and Darius," Brooklynn said. "Start looking!"

At once, the group started to flip switches and turn dials.

But nothing happened.

"None of these are the right buttons," Ben lamented.

"One of them has to be!" Brooklynn said. "I once helped a seamstress find an actual needle in an actual haystack. I can find *this*!"

Kenji kept looking and saw what appeared to be a breaker box on the wall. Pulling it open, he saw a large lever inside. Holding his breath, Kenji threw the lever up.

Suddenly, the room came to life. Lights turned on, computers hummed, monitor screens flickered.

The electricity in Jurassic World was back on. The moment the lever was thrown, electricity zipped through miles and miles of underground wires. Most of the wires led to the various systems that supported the Jurassic World theme park itself—street lights, security systems, rides, theaters, the monorail, and more.

And some of those long wires led to a dark, windowless room far beneath the ground, where fans were whirring away to keep the area cold.

The wires that led into the room continued toward the bottom of a large glass tank.

The lights and the fans suddenly turned on, then turned off just as quickly. The wires attached to the tank sparked.

The room went dark.

Inside the tank, something sat frozen. But with the fans no longer cooling, the temperature started to rise.

A crack could be heard from inside the tank, like ice slowly starting to thaw.

But what was inside the ice?

CHAPTER TWENTY-SIX

Darius and Sammy had managed to hide from Mitch and Tiff so far, but they knew their luck couldn't last forever. It was Darius's turn to carry the weapons bag, and he shouldered it as they made a break for the exit. As they neared the edge of Main Street, they could see the jungle. Another few steps and—

"Having a *Jurassic* day! Don't forget, all pastries are half off after four at Cafe Tricera-muffin-tops, located next to the Lagoon."

The kids stared at each other as if to say, "How did that *happen*?!"

Then the large lights on Main Street turned on. The light was blinding after so long without electricity, and Darius dropped the duffel bag. They shielded their eyes, unaware that Mitch and Tiff were right across the street!

"You guys! Look!" Yasmina shouted as she pointed at a monitor. There were Darius and Sammy standing on Main Street. The kids let out a loud cheer, overjoyed to see their friends again.

But the smiles faded when Mitch and Tiff appeared on the monitor.

"Darius! Sammy! Behind you!" Brooklynn shouted.

"Save your breath," Ben said, shaking his head. "They can't hear us!"

"Where's the stupid speaker button?" Brooklynn said, searching.

The kids started pushing every button in sight, hoping to find the one that activated the Park's PA system.

"Wave if you can hear us!" Yasmina shouted hopefully into a speaker.

"It's over," Tiff said, advancing on the kids. "Don't even think about running."

"Where did you think you were going?" Mitch taunted. "You think we wouldn't be able to find you in the jungle?"

“This isn’t a game, children,” Tiff said, fuming. “Give. Me. The. Weapons.”

“We can’t let you shoot dinosaurs,” Darius said.

“That’s not really your call, is it?” Mitch said, holding out his hands. “Give me the weapons, D. I’m not ask—”

Before he could finish, a beeping sound came from Tiff’s pocket. She reached in and pulled out the ACU tablet.

“Whoever turned on the power, thank you!” Tiff said. She looked at the screen, which once again displayed a map of the Park, indicating a small body of water. There were clusters of dots around the water.

“Guess we don’t need you to show us where the watering hole is after all,” Mitch said.

Darius got a look at the screen as well and noticed a blue dot, separate from the others. It was closing in on Main Street.

“We have to go,” Darius said quietly.

THUMP.

The ground shook.

“We have to go *now,*” Darius whispered with more urgency.

But it was already too late. The group turned around only to see the T. rex advancing on them, growling, opening her mouth, baring her teeth.

She could tell that prey was in her territory. And she was hungry.

CHAPTER TWENTY-SEVEN

What happened next was a blur. Mitch lunged for the weapons bag, fighting Darius, who struggled to hold on. Mitch managed to get it, but Sammy snatched it back. Tiff was rooted to her spot, staring at the T. rex as it stalked closer and closer.

Mitch finally grabbed the bag of weapons away from Sammy, but Darius tackled him.

Then the T. rex roared, charging ahead.

Mitch and Tiff were frightened beyond words and too scared to do anything. That gave Darius and Sammy the chance to grab the weapons and take off.

But Mitch and Tiff recovered and chased after the kids. They caught up quickly and shoved them aside. The weapons bag slid across the street. Darius and Sammy tried to get it, but Mitch and Tiff were too fast—they got to the duffel bag first.

Picking it up, they ran toward the exit.

That left Darius and Sammy stranded on Main Street, with the T. rex headed their way.

"Come on, get up!" Yasmina muttered to the screen.

"There's gotta be another way we can help!" Brooklynn said.

Kenji was busy reading the labels beneath the various systems. "Fence controls, automatic advertising loop, hologram . . . ?"

"How is that going to help them?" Ben asked.

Brooklynn searched the control panels as well. Pounding on a button, she flinched as more Main Street pathway lights came on.

That gave her an idea. . . .

Darius and Sammy were running from the T. rex. They reached a fork in the pathway.

"Which way?" Sammy asked, out of breath.

Darius wasn't sure, nodding in both directions, unable to decide. Suddenly, a light on the pathway flickered on. Then another. And another.

"Follow the lights!" Darius said, realizing that

someone must be turning them on. "They're leading us out!"

The kids continued down Main Street, following the lights as the came on one after another.

They were almost at the gift shop now, with the T. rex gaining ground. Just as they reached it, Darius and Sammy were startled by another blue T. rex that had suddenly appeared in front of them!

The kids kept on running, though—both realized exactly what it was, and they ran right through it.

It was a hologram!

While the kids weren't fooled, the real T. rex was. Confused, she stopped in her tracks, staring at her blue doppelgänger.

Darius and Sammy continued to run. They made it to the jungle as the two T. rexes roared at each other.

"Did that really just happen?" Sammy asked. "Did we actually make it out alive?"

"Uh, yeah," Darius said. "But the lights were *definitely* not part of the plan."

Their attention was quickly drawn to a speaker above them, and the voice that said, "Testing. Testing."

It was Kenji!

"Party people, what WHAAAAAAT?" Kenji

cried out over the loudspeaker.

"You guys! Where are you?" Sammy shouted.

"We found a backup generator and turned the power back on," Brooklynn said over the PA.

From inside the emergency control center, Brooklynn watched as Darius and Sammy waved their hands.

"We can't hear you," Brooklynn said into the speaker. "What are you trying to say? What happened to Tiff and Mitch?"

Sammy shouted again, pointing at something.

"Still can't hear you! Act it out!"

Brooklynn watched curiously as Sammy and Darius were . . . what? Pretending to . . . drink water, was it?

"Okay, uh, TV shows?" Kenji said as if they were playing charades. "Books. A song!"

"They're drinking water!" Ben said.

"The watering hole!" Brooklynn gasped. "They're going to the watering hole!"

Both Darius and Sammy nodded as the two mimed holding weapons.

"They're going to kill the dinosaurs," Brooklynn said softly.

CHAPTER TWENTY-EIGHT

"You guys and Sammy take the boat while I go stop Mitch and Tiff!" Darius said.

"Absolutely not!" Sammy said. "You're going to get killed if you go it alone!"

"I have to! This is all *my* fault! The only reason Mitch and Tiff know about the watering hole is because I showed them. *I'm* the one who didn't listen to Brooklynn. The dinosaurs are in danger because of *me.* I promised everyone that I'd get you home. And I . . . I already lost Ben."

Sammy tried to think of something she could say to get Darius to stay, but she came up empty.

"Hap said their boat is at the northwest dock. Get everyone together and get off the island now, while Mitch and Tiff are busy."

The PA came to life again, but this time, it wasn't Brooklynn or Kenji talking.

"We got your back, Darius! Forget the boat—

Mitch and Tiff are going down!"

"Ben?!" Darius said.

"You're alive?!" Sammy shouted.

"Oh, *riiiiight,*" Ben said. "You didn't know. Yeah. Also, we found the sound button, so we can hear you."

Sammy and Darius, overcome by the joy of learning Ben was alive, hugged each other.

"We're not going to let you do this alone," Brooklynn said. "We're in."

"You don't get it," Darius said. "You guys could get to the boat, save yourselves!"

"You don't get it," Yasmina said over the PA. "You're one of us."

"And we're not going to let Mitch and Tiff get away with killing dinosaurs," Brooklynn finished. "And if they're going to the watering hole to kill dinosaurs . . ."

Darius immediately understood what Brooklynn was getting at. "Then we just have to make sure there aren't any dinosaurs there for them to kill!"

Kenji was steering the motorcycle, trying to balance the bike with both Darius and Sammy behind him. They were all wearing helmets, which was a good thing, because the way Kenji was driving, they were surely going to hit the ground.

"Guys!" Brooklynn shouted over the PA, her voice coming from a speaker behind a rock. "Tiff and Mitch are about to get to the watering hole, and Ben and Yaz aren't there yet!"

Ben and Yaz had taken a still-functioning 6x4 from the command center. If their plan was going to work, it required all the vehicles to be at the watering hole at the same time.

"How far away is the nearest tunnel?" Darius asked as Kenji stopped the bike.

"If you go back the way you came a bit, there's a tunnel entrance that would put you out in front of them," Brooklynn said. She'd remained behind in the emergency control room to help direct the plan.

Darius jumped off the bike. "You guys keep going to the watering hole. Meet up with Ben and Yaz like we planned. You'll move faster without three kids on one bike. I'll slow Mitch and Tiff down."

"Good luck, Dino Nerd!" Kenji said.

The motorcycle took off as Darius opened the tunnel entrance.

"Okay, Darius, what's the plan?" Brooklynn

said. "How can I help? Darius? Darius?"

"Once this is done, get everyone out. Get them home."

Darius slid down the ladder and into the tunnel.

"You noble dummy!" Brooklynn said, shaking her head as she watched Darius on the monitor. "You don't have a plan, do you? You're still trying to go it alone."

Brooklynn didn't know what to do, but she knew she had to help—she couldn't let Darius do this by himself. She got up from her command console and looked at the monitors. One of them showed the vehicle room where Yasmina and Ben had taken the 6x4.

She saw a damaged gyrosphere.

But on another monitor, she saw a long hallway labeled E-750.

The number on the envelope she had found back at the genetics lab. The number she had seen on Dr. Wu's computer. The mysterious number she had been trying to decode for weeks.

Brooklynn had a choice to make.

CHAPTER TWENTY-NINE

The sun had just appeared above the horizon as Mitch checked the ACU tablet. He and Tiff were nearly at the watering hole. And judging by all the little dots surrounding it, there was a full house.

Tiff hacked away at plants with a machete, swatting away mosquitoes and muttering under her breath. As she slashed away the last bush, she expected to see the watering hole.

And she did.

Except, blocking her path was an unarmed Darius.

"Hey, guys," he said. "How's the vacation shaping up?"

"I assumed the T. rex would eat you," Tiff said, rolling her eyes. "But I guess she has taste."

"Get out of the way, D," Mitch said. "Be smart about this. The rest of your friends are dead-weight, but you can still get out of here."

But Darius held his ground. "No. I'm gonna save them. And I'm gonna stop you. Whatever it takes."

"I liked you, Darius," Mitch said, holding his rifle. "You're a smart kid, but you can't have it both ways. I told you you'd have to choose, and you made the wrong—"

Before he could finish, a damaged gyrosphere exploded out of the jungle, spinning wildly, its gears grinding loudly. The ball hurtled to a stop right by Darius. The door opened, and Brooklynn stood beside Darius.

"What the heck are you doing?" she said angrily. "I thought we were a team!"

"I couldn't put you guys in more danger," he said. "This is my fault."

"No, Darius, you have been trying to get us home since the moment the Indominus rex broke out. The only thing you're guilty of is keeping us all alive. And I'm sorry it took me this long to say that."

Darius shook his head. "No, I'm sorry. You were right to be suspicious."

The two smiled at each other as Tiff yelled, "Hey!"

The two kids turned and saw Tiff waving her rifle in the air. "What is— We have guns! We're threatening you!"

"So, has this gone on long enough?" Darius asked.

"I'd say *just* long enough!" Brooklynn answered.

Mitch and Tiff exchanged puzzled looks as they watched the dinosaurs gathering around the watering hole. There were grazing Sinoceratops, a Parasaurolophus, a Ceratosaurus, some Compsognathuses, and a 6x4.

Well, the 6x4 wasn't a dino—it was a vehicle driven by Yasmina. She was driving alongside Ben, who was riding atop Bumpy, waving flashlights.

"Here! Here!" Ben shouted.

The flashlights got the attention of Pteranodons flying above. They began following Ben.

Now the dinosaurs at the watering hole went wild! The Ceratosaurus roared as several Pteranodons dive-bombed it and the other creatures.

The dinosaurs started to run.

CHAPTER THIRTY

The plan was working! The kids had distracted the dinosaurs, who were now stampeding away from the watering hole and, most importantly, Mitch and Tiff.

Yasmina stopped the 6x4, and Kenji pulled up alongside on the motorcycle. They watched as the dinosaurs continued to run, far away from the watering hole now.

Everything was great, except Bumpy started to bellow, stepping in front of Ben. She raised her tail, ready to strike.

Ben looked over at the edge of the jungle and grimaced. "Guys . . . ," he said.

As a lone Parasaurolophus screeched at a diving Pteranodon, the T. rex burst out of the jungle. It knocked the Pteranodon out of the air, and the flying reptile skidded along the ground.

The Parasaurolophus turned to run away, and

the kids gasped as they saw the dinosaur herd coming right back toward them!

Yasmina sprinted for the 6x4 and hopped in. “Ben, let’s go!” she shouted.

But Ben ran to the driver’s side and hauled Yasmina out of the vehicle just as a Sinoceratops slammed into it.

The dinosaur stampede was all around them, and Bumpy did her best to protect her friends with her tail.

The ground rumbled as Darius and Brooklynn hopped into the gyrosphere. But it wouldn’t start! Mitch and Tiff watched as a Stegosaurus approached the kids and ran off into the jungle.

The Stegosaurus rammed into the gyrosphere, jump-starting the engine. Brooklynn and Darius both grabbed the joystick, and the vehicle took off!

Mitch and Tiff were running at full speed, terrified of being flattened by the oncoming crush of dinosaurs. The ground rumbled beneath their feet as they ditched the duffel bag to lighten their load.

They saw a low-hanging branch up ahead, and Tiff grabbed it, swinging herself up into the tree. Mitch was only a second behind her. If they'd been any slower, the dinosaurs would have run right into them. As it was, the dinosaurs thundered beneath the tree, shearing off some lower branches.

The dinosaurs caused the tree to vibrate, and Tiff lost control of her rifle. It fell to the ground and was promptly trampled. When the herd had finally passed, the "ecotourists" climbed out of the tree. To say Tiff's rifle was beyond use was an understatement. It was utterly destroyed.

"No, no, no!" she screamed.

"Leave it and come on!" Mitch shouted. "At this point, we just need to get back to the boat before—WHOA!!!"

Mitch had shifted his step, and something closed around his foot, yanking him up into the air. He was now hanging upside down from a tree branch, swaying back and forth.

"Oh, that's right," Tiff said with a sneer. "You set all those traps earlier, didn't you? They were going to help you catch dinosaurs, weren't they?"

"Get me out of this!" Mitch screamed.

Tiff tried to get hold of Mitch, to get him to stop swaying. "Hold still!"

“Uh, gee, Tiff,” Mitch said sarcastically. “I can’t, for some reason! Maybe it’s because I’m in one of our snare traps!”

“Well, I’m sorry you forgot where you and Hap set it!”

Before the two could continue their argument, a mighty roar came from the jungle. And it was getting closer. The T. rex!

A horde of Compys came running from the underbrush, and by now Mitch and Tiff knew this was a terrible sign. A moment later, the T. rex emerged, its jaws open, snarling.

“Hurry!” Mitch screamed.

The T. rex roared again, and Mitch swayed from the tree.

Then Tiff grabbed Mitch’s gun, and put her hands in his pocket—removing a set of keys.

“Babe?” Mitch said.

“I’ve never liked that nickname!” she yelled as she ran away, leaving Mitch to the mercy of the T. rex.

CHAPTER THIRTY-ONE

The gyrosphere rolled to a halt near the docks as the sun beat down on the jungle below. Smoke filled the Plexiglas ball as Darius and Brooklynn jumped out. They coughed and looked at their surroundings.

In the distance, at the edge of the dock, they could see it—Mitch and Tiff's yacht.

With Tiff standing on the deck.

"I win!" she shouted, gloating. "I'm out of here! I got the boat, and you're *never* getting off this awful, awful island!"

Darius and Brooklynn sprinted toward the dock, but they were too late. They would never reach Tiff in time, as the yacht had already begun to drift away from the pier. Tiff disappeared inside and emerged at the top of the boat, by the captain's chair.

"In fact, I'm going back, and I'm not telling *anyone* that you're here!" Tiff shouted. "You are going to *rot* here for all eternity—if the dinosaurs don't get you first!"

Darius watched as the yacht started to shimmy in the water, almost as if something had just jumped aboard—but he couldn't see anything.

Tiff gave the engine some gas, and the boat dipped in the water slightly as it raced off.

A chill went up Darius's spine as he realized what had happened. Brooklynn realized it, too.

They both waved their arms wildly, jumping up and down, trying to get Tiff's attention. "Stop!" they shouted. "Stop! You gotta get off the boat!"

Tiff was too busy feeling superior. She didn't even look back as she said, "Stoooooop, come baaaaack!" Then she laughed. "No one tells *me* no. No one gets in my way. You ruined my vacation. My marriage. And my best gun. You are *never* going home!"

She looked down at her pink neckerchief, straightening it. When she looked back up, she didn't see open ocean. Instead, all she saw were Baryonyxes.

The dinosaurs jumped at Tiff.

Back on the dock, Darius and Brooklynn could only watch in horror as the boat sailed out of sight. They knew what was going to happen to Tiff. They did not wish it on her. In fact, it felt like the whole island was that boat, and the dinosaurs were coming for them, too.

CHAPTER THIRTY-TWO

The motorcycle roared out of the jungle and toward the dock, its engine sputtering. It was followed closely by Ben and Bumpy.

"Hey," Ben said, raising his hand.

Darius ran over to his friend and wrapped him up in the biggest hug. Ben smiled and hugged Darius right back.

"I'm sorry," Darius said. "I tried to hold on—"

"I missed you guys, too," Ben replied.

Before Darius could break the hug, Brooklynn jumped in and hugged them both. They were quickly joined by Kenji, then Yasmina, and at last, Sammy.

"Starting . . . to lose . . . air . . . ," Yasmina croaked.

They laughed and broke the hug.

"So . . . what now?" Kenji asked. "Try to find another distress beacon?"

"No," Darius said. "We're done waiting for

someone to rescue us. It's time we found our *own* way off the island. . . ."

The group smiled at Darius, and he grinned right back.

"Besides, I don't think anyone got our signal anyway."

EPILOGUE

Meanwhile, deep in the jungle, at Dr. Wu's secret lab, something was stirring. The dull thumping sound of flesh hammering against steel and reinforced glass echoed in the darkness. Sharp talons scratched at the enclosure as cold fog poured out of the deactivated machinery that had kept the now-awakened thing in icy suspended animation. Suddenly, the glass shattered, and the creature let out a horrifying screech to let the world know it was free!

JURASSIC WORLD

CAMP CRETACEOUS